The Diamond Head Deception

james blakley

the Diamond Head Deception

Thanks to God for everything. First, for giving me a wonderful, hard-working family, who raised me, supported me when I was nothing, and encouraged me to achieve my first feat of fiction. For the blessing of tremendously talented teachers, professors, friends, and colleagues who helped broaden my mind. For the flair for fiction and for the guts to go where I've had to in order to make it grow. And finally, for three great states among the fabulous fifty: Missouri (where I learned what I know); Kansas (where I've used it to survive); and Oregon (where Inkwater Press's top-notch editing, production design, and customer service assistance to The Powers That Be Publishing has given me the opportunity to thrive).

"No man is an island, entire of itself. Every man is a piece of the continent, a part of the main."

--John Donne (Meditation XVII)

"The Devil hath power to assume a pleasing shape."

–William Shakespeare, Hamlet Act 2, scene 2

Contents

CHAPTER 1

Out to Pasture

The summer's biggest event, the Fourth of July, had fizzled. And until the start of football and the end of baseball in September, there wouldn't be much to get fired up about. The only light show now came from the sun: It scorched the Lower Forty-Eight with intense temperatures for often weeks on end. And few places had it worse than the Midwest. But in Iowa, Corn Country Carnival Days was a way to beat the heat. In the middle of what was usually nowhere was a sprawl of cooled tents and booths (each filled with games to play and things to buy). And nearby were the twists and turns of a Ferris wheel, a rollercoaster, and a carousel ride—all nice distractions.

But for some, the carnival wasn't just a retreat from the heat: They had business there. Some of it was legal, some illegal. For the criminal set, the tents could provide cover from a satellite sweep; and the crowd, ample alibis to cover their butts.

Barnabas "Barney" Aikers sat munching on his second deep-fried Twinkie in the parking lot. The gray-haired, sixty-something farmer looked like he'd had a few too many of them lately, as his overalls strained to contain a bloated belly. But he licked his fingers too soon because, from his truck, he spotted another dish walking up. Since he'd eaten dessert already, Barney didn't feast his eyes on the petite young lady's strawberry blonde locks, cherry-red lips, and cornflower-blue eyes. Instead, he locked onto her big picnic basket, wondering if it contained the main course.

The strawberry blonde waved. "Hi, Mr. Aikers," her high-pitched voice greeted Barney.

The farmer piled out of his pickup. He mimicked the strawberry blonde's smile and tipped his hat in gentlemanly fashion. "How-do, little lady?" he asked.

"Jim-dandy," she answered.

"Your uncle don't take a shine to the jubilee no more, and sent you to do his bidding, huh?"

"It's my foster daddy, I told you," the strawberry blonde laughed.

"Pardon me. I forget a lot lately; got a lot on my mind, you understand."

"Daddy's busy, getting back up on his feet from the drought. He wants to know—everybody does, really— how you did it: How you made so much with so few bushels?"

"Ever hear that Bible story about Jesus Christ and the five loaves and fishes?"

"Yes, sir."

"Well, not me! I don't just give out my special recipe for success for nothing, see?"

"Yes, sir. That's why us gals whipped up some of our home cooking for you, Mr. Aikers."

Barney's eyes widened and he licked his lips. "Is that what you got there in your basket?"

The strawberry blonde nodded.

"Mind if I have me a look-see?"

The strawberry blonde lifted the checkered cloth and Barney peeked inside. His mouth watered and a broad smile blossomed at the sight of a basketful of bundled one hundred dollar bills. "Greens," the strawberry blonde announced. "You like, Mr. Aikers?"

"*Yum-yum, give me some!*" Barney hooted. "But I don't want to sample it out here. Too many...*bugs*. Suppose we go over yonder there to..."

The sound began to crackle and fade through the headset of young Seymore Eaves. "*Oy vey!*" he complained, pounding his forehead.

Luna Nightcrow recognized the Yiddish expression of dismay and wondered what caused it. But when she moved forward to find out, she was almost on top of Eaves! The United States Department of

Agriculture surveillance van she sat in was small, devoted to mostly equipment. For Eaves, having an older woman like Luna pressed against him would usually be a dream come true. But now, she only smothered him with concern. "What's wrong?" Luna wanted to know.

"Charly's—I mean, Clover Fields's—play-acting, that's what!" Eaves griped, readjusting his headset and the sound. "All that playing, swaying, and sweating is messing up the audio..."

Luna grabbed the van's second headset and pressed it to her ear. It took a few minutes for the sound to pick up. When it did, Luna heard the strawberry blonde called "Clover Fields" say, "*Wow! The hog tent! Are you wanting to add some fatback to your greens, Mr. Aikers?*"

"Nah," Barney said. Then, wildness flashed across the farmer's face. "I want to make you feel right at home." Fields felt the presence of some-thing—of someone—else. A lanky, red-bearded man in a baseball cap had slipped in behind. Clover Fields was suddenly sandwiched.

"So, missy, ole Barney tells me that you like to squeal," Fields heard the man say.

A shower of static drowned further transmis-sion. But Eaves heard enough. "*Oh, shit! Her cover is blown!*" He turned around, but found that he was the only one in the surveillance van.

After hearing Barney lure Fields to the tent, Luna

detected the danger and jumped from the parking lot blind. She quickly made it to the carnival grounds, but the crowd slowed her roll. About ten minutes later, the insurance investigator finally found the green-and-brown-striped hog tent. Luna approached the ticket booth. A hand-written "gone to lunch" sign plastered the window, but Luna saw a portable fan still running inside. Ever suspicious, she raised her T-shirt, unsnapped her Flash Bang holster, and released a snub-nosed .38. Luna tucked it in the waistband of her jeans, and removed her Sony Xperia smartphone. She turned on the LED flashlight app. The phone changed into a bar of blazing light that Luna raised with one hand, while drawing her handgun with the other. Cautiously she stepped inside the tent.

It was dim and reeked of round up swine. *"Fields?"* Luna called. Oinks were the only reply. Suddenly, Luna saw something. On the ground, a few feet ahead, was a body. She moved swiftly, her gun ready. The flashlight revealed the glassy stare of an elderly man. Not a fat one, but thin and bald instead. Luna kneeled and felt his neck for a pulse. Sadly, there was none. She stood and prepared to move forward, but turned into what felt like a stump. Luna stumbled backward in shock, her smartphone flying from her hand. When she looked up, standing in front of her was a human shape. Luna raised her gun. But before she could squeeze off a shot, the shadowy profile began to fall forward. Luna rolled out of the way, as it hit the ground face-first.

The insurance investigator found her smartphone and turned the fallen figure over. A burst of white flashlight uncovered… *Charly!* Luna gasped. It was USDA Risk Management Special Agent Charlene "Charly" Barns (alias Clover Fields).

"Luna? S-sorry…," Barns mumbled. "…should've stayed…desk work."

Barns managed to cover herself with the tattered remnants of her dress. It had been torn off by her attackers. But, there wasn't a clunky, old-fashioned wire to find taped to her torso. They missed the tiny digital microphone (still hidden in the Special Agent's ring).

But, a bullet from the attackers didn't miss: Luna noticed blood welling up from a point-blank gunshot wound just below Barns's exposed shoulder. "You did just fine, Charly," Luna reassured the Special Agent. She then pressed her earphone and shouted into her mini-mike, *"This's Luna to Eaves, over!"* Luna heard only static. She returned her attention to Barns. "The elderly man: Was he..?"

Barns shook her head. "Ticket taker, not one of them," she said. "…took my gun. They tried to make it look like…" The Special Agent groaned and pitched forward; her shoulder felt like it was on fire.

Luna helped Barns lay back. Then gently she asked her, "They: Barney and who, Charly?"

Barns fought for self-control, but lost it again. *"God, it hurts!* Those male chauvinist..."

Luna forced a smile. "Don't say it."

"...pigs!" the Special Agent blurted.

"What men aren't?" Luna asked.

"Milo, my husband..." With that, Barns grabbed Luna's arm and snarled, *"Get them!"*

Luna tore a strip off Barns's dress, balled it, and placed it over the gunshot wound. She triggered her smartphone location services signal and sat the device beside the shivering Special Agent. Luna stood, tucked her .38 into the hip pocket of her jeans, and left the tent. Once outside, she looked around. But by now, Aikers and his accomplice were probably long gone. Luna passed a packed John Deere farm equipment display when suddenly, she grabbed her ear in pain. *"Dammit, Seymore!"* Luna yelled, as the earphone finally buzzed loudly to life.

The surveillance tech fiddled with the volume control. "Sorry," his voice returned.

Luna raised her mike. "Charly's hit and I've lost Aikers and somebody else!" she reported.

"I'll alert medical! Who else are you tracking, besides Aikers?"

"I don't know. Any sign of Aikers in the parking lot?"

Eaves downloaded an aerial satellite image of the parking lots, isolated Barney's pickup truck, and zoomed in. Finally, the surveillance tech reported, "Negative, but I'll keep looking."

Luna decided to play a hunch. She remembered the report on Barney: The only thing he likes to grow is his gut. *He probably thinks he's in the clear, and is parked at a concession stand!* Luna thought. Her eyes frantically scanned the food lines for the fat man, but saw too many that might fit his description. Then something else grabbed her attention: A man wearing a dark, satiny windbreaker...*on a 92-degree day?!* Luna saw him near the barbeque hut. By the time she got close, the man was gone. But maybe he led her to... *Aikers!* Luna thought she saw him: An old man in overalls with a beer belly. However, a straw hat shaded his face. She had to get closer.

The fat man in the straw hat didn't appear to see Luna. But as she closed in, a sudden stream of people again blocked her view. When they passed, the fat man in the straw hat reappeared. Only now, he had select company: A man wearing a shiny, black windbreaker and a ball cap. And when he turned, he locked a set of beady eyes directly on Luna's long, dark hair and cinnamon-colored complexion. In a sea of overwhelming whiteness, she was a giveaway. And when the man in the black jacket (named Clyde Tiller) tapped his fat friend's shoulder, it was time to get away.

Barney Aikers dropped his plate of ribs, picked up the pilfered picnic basket, and hurried into the crowd.

Luna shouted, *"BARNEY!"*, and gave chase. The fat farmer vanished into another tent. Before Luna could follow, the tent flap flew up. Clyde Tiller appeared. Without breaking a sweat, he dipped his hand into his jacket, drew a semi-automatic, and then opened fire. Instead of Luna, a passerby took the first bullet. His shriek turned the festivities into a stampede for safety. Luna dove behind a bale of hay, as more slugs whizzed her way. When the shots stopped, Luna peeked up. She saw Tiller make for the carousel. Luna readied her gun and started to run.

Suddenly, gunfire burst from the ride. Luna screamed, grabbed her side, and staggered to the ground. When the carousel made a full turn, Tiller jumped off. He saw the female body ahead, but still approached cautiously to make sure it was dead. Tiller got to within a few feet of Luna. Still, there was no movement. The bearded man reached into his jeans pocket for a magazine to reload. But Tiller's slowness of pace was a mistake. Luna leaped to life and raised her revolver.

Tiller's eyes widened. *"What in the Sam Hill..?"* was all he got out of his mouth.

Luna answered Tiller's question with a single shot. *BAM!* The gun lurched, causing the bullet to go lower than Luna intended. It connected with the bearded man's crotch. Tiller yelped, from the excruciating pain, and collapsed into a squirming ball. Luna took his gun and started to run. But she stopped, looked back, and shouted, *"For Fields!"*

Luna hurried back to the tent that she'd seen Barney run inside. Instead of going in, she went around the side. The insurance investigator knelt and saw a few boot prints in the dirt. When Luna looked up, she saw Barney in the distance. He was fleeing the carnival! Suddenly, Luna remembered seeing something that might help catch him. She ran back to the empty grounds.

Barney Aikers stopped for a moment. He finally caught his breath and looked around. "No more screams from the crowd. *I got it made!"* he chuckled.

Suddenly, there was a *BOOM!* It wasn't from thunder, but from concession stands crumbling under the massive weight of a 6R Series John Deere tractor. And behind the wheel was the insatiable insurance sleuth Luna Nightcrow. Barney screamed and ran for what he hoped was the cover of a nearby cornfield. But Luna saw him, switched gears, and plowed through in pursuit.

Barney dived to his right and barely avoided being trampled. The tractor rumbled forward, leaving him to scrabble for escape. Barney swiped and swatted away the stinging, stabbing seven-foot tall stalks. Suddenly, he staggered and fell. Barney ripped the table cloth from the picnic basket and stuffed as much cash into his overalls as he could. Then, he crawled on his knees for what felt like a mile. He couldn't hear the tractor engine anymore, just his own wheezing.

Barney asked himself, *Was paying crop inspector Clyde Tiller to fake damage to my crops worth this?! And me, selling the real production under a fake name!* Maybe, his conscience told him. Maybe, I can get a high-priced lawyer to cook me up an entrapment defense. Or maybe, I can get a jury to believe that crazy Cherokee crop cop tried to kill me, instead of talk to me. *Yeah!* There have to be some witnesses to the tractor she stole and the damage she did with it.

Building himself a defense case sped up Barney's pace. And things looked even better, when flickers of sunlight filtered through the canopy of corn. Barney could see a clearing ahead. He got to his feet, dusted himself off, and walked toward it. About 10 minutes passed, but at last Barney cleared the field! He was home-free. That is, if he could get past the several tons of metal (molded into fast-moving farm machinery) parked a few yards ahead. *Fat chance!* Luna Nightcrow emerged from the tractor cab and trained her revolver on a beaten Barney.

"Luna, come in!" It was Seymore Eaves in her ear. "Everything okay? Where's Aikers?"

Luna pressed her earphone and grinned. "Out to pasture," she answered.

ALMOST ONE YEAR LATER …

CHAPTER 2

Last of Her Kind

After all these years, you're getting an once-in-a-lifetime break, the middle-aged man told himself. *A chance at greatness—perhaps even immortality!*

The middle-aged man's ratty, scrawny reflection bounced back at him from the Ray-Ban shades of the smiling, dark-haired local in front of him. The local wore a white, short-sleeve shirt; tan, cotton pants; and loafers. But, it was his offer that most impressed the middle-aged man: "Many people are going to remember this moment. It's a shot for not only you, but your people, to be seen!"

The middle-aged man could take the local's $500 upfront and run. But ultimately, whereto? The greater possibilities were too big to pass up. So, the middle-aged man left a street life of panhandling behind—for good, he hoped—and confidently approached the wharf. He lugged the duffel bag, given to him by the convincing local, down the rickety ladder to the water and an awaiting motorboat.

The engine soon started. *Bigger things are on the horizon!* the local's words echoed through the middle-aged man's mind, as he set out.

··◆··

The Shilpa was the last of her kind. Heavy, thick, and strong, she was built for safe and swift sailing, not to be a floating fantasy land that was piled high with theme park pleasures. Yes, there was a bar, dining room, casino, and a sizeable swimming pool to keep her 200 passengers entertained. But, the ocean liner possessed an old style elegance that Rupert "Rupee" Sabal enjoyed. He liked the twin blue smoke stacks crowning *The Shilpa* and the navy blue band around her white hull. And the sound of her bow plowing through the turquoise-tinted sea with a constant *swish* was calming. It reminded Rupee of the ships he saw in picture books as a boy, and could now afford to travel onboard comfortably as an accomplished man.

Rupee finished a game of twenty-one and left the casino for his state room. Inside, he gathered his cricket bag and strolled topside. Rupee was below so long that day had almost turned into night. The sun was red and low—tired and just about tucked into a blanket of purple clouds that hung over the horizon. Rupee hauled his bag towards the bow. He could barely see the famous dorsal fin ridge of Diamond Head Crater in the distance. And curving out from it for miles were the welcoming, beachfront twinkles of "The Town" (as the locals called it). *The Shilpa* slowed as the paradise port of Honolulu called.

Rupee hoped to get in a few cricket moves with his practice partner, before docking. He checked his Rolex; his partner should be there. Rupee shrugged, wrenched his bow tie free, and undid his dinner jacket. He waited, taking in the fragrance of the tropics. Though he smelled it just 6 months ago, the exciting, overseas breeze carried away the stench of cigars and soothed the sting of losing at cards. But what Rupee felt next was anything but relaxing.

BANG! The ship rumbled and shook. The cricketer lost his footing. Is this one of those deep sea earthquakes I read about? he thought. Rupee picked himself off the deck. His first thought was to get below, to the security office. But, a flood of passengers quickly clogged the decks. Most of them were focused on something in the water. Rupee pushed his way through the throng for a look. Not far from the ship, a white-clad body floated face down. All of a sudden, a distant buzzing captured everyone's ears. It had to be the sound of an outboard motor—*rescue!*

Before Rupee could see another vessel, he felt the ship that he was on shake. Then, there was another loud noise, even more frightening than the first one Rupee heard. It was the emergency alarms wailing.

Was *The Shilpa* sinking? When the crew appeared, and then issued evacuation orders, it was official: *The Shilpa* was sinking. But how, when she was so heavy, thick, and strong?

Meanwhile, the buzzing proved to be the sound of a small motorboat. Everyone saw it stop several yards short of running alongside the ocean liner. Its occupant, the middle-aged man hoping for fame and fortune, stood and raised his arms. But it wasn't to hail the ship; it was to hoist something onto his shoulder, instead. But it wasn't to hail the ship; it was to hoist something onto his shoulder, instead. Suddenly, the night became day when a screaming, white-hot stream of gas hurled a rocket *The Shilpa*'s way.

The ship began to lean, and everyone saw the dark ocean rise onto the lower deck. The captain appeared from the bridge and saw the lifeboats being manned and lowered into the ocean. He worried that the Mayday messages he sent would take all day for someone to hear. Then, the ocean was brightened by more explosions. But this time, the fire rained from above, from the mounted machine gun of an unidentified helicopter. It riddled the motorboat with bullets, and within a minute there was one less ship on the sea (as the motorboat blew apart violently). *Someone heard the captain's Mayday and saved the day!* But sadly, they couldn't save *The Shilpa;* she was taking on water fast.

Rupee turned from the railing and tried to make

it below. But a short, stocky woman stopped him. "Where are you going?" she wanted to know.

"Below!" Rupee shouted. "I must…"

"You must get into the lifeboat, sir!" the stocky woman insisted, blocking Rupee's path.

Rupee pushed through the woman's bulk, but couldn't budge that of a tall, muscular passenger standing behind her. The man's glare was enough to repel Rupee, but he didn't leave it to chance. The man added a push that knocked the cricketer back to the railing. This time, Rupee didn't move or even look back. He waited to be helped into one of several lifeboats below.

Drifting a couple of hours aboard one of the cramped, partially-enclosed lifeboats seemed like a day at sea. But Rupee and two hundred or so of his fellow passengers were safe. And the situation really improved, when a U.S. Coast Guard cutter finally arrived on scene. But suddenly, there were gasps from onboard Rupee's lifeboat. Then a soft, but firm, hand landed on his shoulder. Rupee turned to see that it was the woman who stopped him from returning below deck.

"I heard the cries," Rupee said to her. "It must mean that *Shilpa..?*"

The stocky woman nodded. "Yes, it has sunk," she confirmed.

Rupee nodded. For a moment, his head dropped. He then looked up. "I might have sunk too, had it not been for you. Thank you, Ms. Aapt," he told the woman.

The woman named "Aapt" replied stoically, "It was my duty, Mr. Sabal."

If only he hadn't gambled, Rupee could have saved more than his life. He clutched his cricket bag, praying that it would save him again. Because having lost $50,000 playing cards, and now Pacific Splendor, what else was there in life?

CHAPTER 3

Cornfield Comeuppance

"In the first count of federal crop insurance fraud, how do you find the defendant?"

"We, the jury, find the defendant guilty, your honor," the jury foreman told the judge.

"In the second count of assaulting a federal officer, how do you find the defendant?"

"We, the jury, find the defendant guilty, your honor."

And so went the fluid back-and-forth between judge and jury through several more counts against Barney Aikers. His accomplice, Clyde Tiller, plea bargained. And, that left ole Barney to battle through court by himself. But now, it was over. The gavel pounded and the emotions of the courtroom crowd sounded. Luna turned and waved to a grateful, young strawberry blonde and her strapping husband. After several months of waiting for the trial, Luna was satisfied. She was happy that Charly pulled through and that Barney and Clyde were through (each headed for the pen).

Luna broke free from the clutch of media microphones and cameras outside the U.S. Courthouse in Cedar Rapids, Iowa. She made it to her rental car and started up. Luna headed south onto Interstate 80 and turned west for Des Moines International Airport (for a late flight home).

It was a cloudy, early summer day, but not nearly as hot as when Luna was last in Iowa. So, she turned off the air and lowered the power windows a bit. The cool breeze refreshed what was a rather dull drive. Luna was from Oklahoma "Green Country" and used to seeing similar rolling, velvety pastures and fields of growing harvests. So after an hour's drive, the S-Class Mercedes with tinted windows that motored behind her was a welcomed change of pace. After the crop fraud case, Luna knew that multi-millions of dollars were tied up in agribusiness. So, the black luxury car didn't seem out of place or suspicious. That is, until she stopped at a red light.

The Mercedes already blew by on yellow. But instead of continuing on, the driver pulled over and waited for the light to turn green. And when Luna started up and sped by, the Mercedes pulled out and soon caught up to her again. When Luna changed lanes, the Mercedes changed lanes. If she slowed, it slowed. Luna began to fear that this was an attempt at revenge (for her testimony against Barney and Clyde). She got the license plate number, picked up her smartphone, and prepared to dial 911. But an all too familiar sound stopped her: The beep of the low battery signal. *Damn!* And by the time she looked up exactly where she was for dispatch (as Luna didn't see any signs ahead) the phone would be dead. I could jumpstart it with my Yellow Jacket stun gun case, Luna quickly thought. But, it will drain the weapon's charge. And, if the cops can't get to me quickly, I need protection. No, it looked like Luna would have to take care of this alone. So, she sped up and changed lanes. The Mercedes took the bait and followed.

Not wanting any civilians to get hurt or killed this time, Luna quickly veered off I-80 and headed back north, along less-crowded Highway 6, taking them deeper into rural Iowa. The Mercedes tailed Luna's Dodge Avenger for almost 15 minutes, giving her time to develop a plan. When one finally came together, Luna peeled off the paved road and rumbled down the gravely lengths of a back road that led toward a cornfield. She spotted a turn-off up ahead and hit the gas. Luna swerved right, kicking up a huge cloud of dust. The Mercedes roared through and screeched to a halt. The driver just missed crashing into cropland. He backed up and then carefully made the same turn as Luna had. The Mercedes travelled slowly down what was now a narrow dirt road. And up ahead, the driver finally spotted Luna's rental car parked off to the side. The Mercedes pulled to within a few feet behind the Dodge Avenger and ground to a stop.

The door to the luxury car opened. Out stepped its driver: A thin black man, dressed in matching black trousers and T-shirt and wreathed with a gold neck chain. He saw nothing but corn to the left of him, corn to the right of him, and no movement from the car ahead. And the only sound was the wind rustling through fields of ripening stalks. Carefully, the driver reached into his pocket. He eased out a shiny .22 caliber pistol and crept toward the driver's side of Luna's car. With his free hand, the man gently reached for the door. Then he swung it open, but was greeted by an empty interior. The driver closed the door and walked around the front of the abandoned vehicle. A few feet from the passenger side, he spotted a pair of women's heels in the grass.

"She must have gone into the field," the driver thought aloud. He prepared to comb through the crops when he sensed something behind him. But he was too slow to react.

Luna sprinted from the opposite field of corn, across the road, and then slammed into the driver with her Yellow Jacket smartphone stun gun. He screamed and fell to his knees, stung by 60,000 volts of electricity. Luna alertly grabbed the driver's .22 from the ground and then the back of his neck chain. The chain drew back hard against the driver's throat, choking him like a tight leash. Luna planted her foot in his back and drove him forward. The driver hit the grass face-first. Luna landed a knee hard against his spine. And the force from her 5'9" frame made him whine.

Then, there was a familiar "click." The driver recognized it as the safety being dropped on his gun. He pleaded, *"Don't shoot, Luna! It's cool, okay? It's cool!"*

"So is the morgue, which is where you're headed, unless you tell me who you are!" she growled.

"Sure, sure!" the driver begged. "Got to get some ID, okay?"

"Don't try anything cute! You hear me?"

"Loud and clear!"

Luna lifted her knee from the driver's back and stood. The driver remained on the ground, recovering. When he got up, Luna immediately pushed him forward and marched him at gunpoint to the Mercedes. The driver reached inside and picked his wallet off the passenger seat.

Luna assumed a firing stance. *"Turn around slowly!"* she ordered. When the driver did, Luna grabbed the wallet from his trembling hand and flipped it open. The face on the Iowa-issued driver's license matched that of the man in front of her, but it couldn't convey his true intentions.

"Uh, I got a business card in there, too," the driver added.

Luna saw an embossed white card in the wallet, and thumbed it up. She read it: "Dré Brand, Executive's Assistant: Continental Property Adjustment."

An apologetic smile filled the driver's face, revealing his youth. "I'm sorry, Luna, but..."

"That's Ms. Nightcrow!"

"My bad, okay? I was sent to find you for my boss. I didn't mean you no harm—for real!"

"Then why the gun, Dré?" Luna wanted to know.

"In case I got to kill more than just time up here," the young man replied. "Look around you, Ms. Nightcrow, we're outnumbered!"

"By what, corn?"

"No, I mean there's not too many brothas or Indians up here," Dré explained. "Besides, the way you was driving so fast, I thought that you was taken hostage or something!"

Luna still looked long and hard at him. "So, you just rode to my rescue, huh?"

"It kind of fits what I want to do someday: Be a recovery agent. You know, find people or..." Dré turned, fetched Luna's shoes, and said, "... their property. Peace, okay?"

Luna lowered the .22, removed the magazine, and tossed it back to Dré. "Peace," she parroted.

"Hey! What about my...?"

"You can have it when we get to Des Moines," Luna said, putting the gun in her pocket.

Dré grinned, pocketed his magazine, and pointed to Luna's smartphone. "That's a pretty convincing conversation piece you got there, Ms. Nightcrow," he said.

"Yeah," Luna agreed. "I keep it handy, in case I need to shoot more than the breeze."

CHAPTER 4

Trouble in Paradise

Luna followed Dré Brand into Des Moines, Iowa—West Des Moines, Iowa, specifically—where Continental Property Adjustment (or CPA) was located. The high-rise complex's mirrored-glass façades gave Luna a chance for a quick look-over before entering. Luckily, she wore her gray skirt suit to court; so the cornfield dirt and dust that Luna didn't get cleaned off sort of blended in. And a quick perfume spritz made her feel 90 percent presentable.

After waiting a few minutes in the lobby, Luna was finally ushered by the secretary into the office of Chief Financial Officer Evelyn Grace. "Darn boy's going get his fool head shot off one of these days!" was Evelyn's reaction to word of the insurance investigator's run-in with the company's Mercedes driver. "I sure hope you knocked some sense into him, Luna!"

"I'm afraid not," Luna sighed. "Still says he wants to be a retriever someday."

Evelyn shook her head. "All he's liable to find is more trouble!" she said.

Evelyn Grace, 54, was a heavy-set black woman with a sparkly smile and a shiny perm. She wore a royal blue pantsuit and her taste in interior decorating was almost as elegant as Dré's style. Luna was most grateful for the presence of an espresso machine. Evelyn fixed her a cup. After one sip, Luna was instantly at ease—so much so, that she forgave Dré. "No harm done," Luna said. "I think I lost 10 pounds, from all the thinking, sweating, and running! And that's probably the most excitement the kid's had, too. Things can be a bit slow-moving up here."

"I'm used to a lot of Iowa; it looks like the Illinois farmland I grew up on, Luna. But Des Moines is Times Square, compared to my hole-in-the-wall hometown. That's why I splurged on these fashionable furnishings!" Evelyn laughed. "Dré, my nephew, hasn't had a chance to adjust yet. He's only a few months off the bus from big city St. Louis, where he was born and raised."

Luna took another sip of espresso. "Which side of the Arch is he from?" she asked.

"The side that grows a bumper crop of bad behavior. So, I did my brother a favor and brought

Dré up here to work for me. He's still a wannabe. But, since a lot of folks up here only see the gangsta image on TV, he comes in handy when Special Investigations needs a little help getting leads on stolen stuff or grilling the crooks who took it. I usually have him run errands. Like today: Dré was just supposed to offer you a chauffeured ride. I should have called you, instead."

Luna smiled. "I forgot to charge my smartphone; so, you may not have gotten me anyway," she remarked. "But you have me now, Evelyn, so what's the problem?"

"I know you've been busy with that crop insurance con, and congrats on helping the feds close it," the CFO began. "But, you may not be up on what's going down elsewhere."

"I was a witness, Evelyn, not a juror."

"Sorry, Luna." Evelyn then settled into the seat behind her desk. "What do you know about diamonds?"

"Not as much as investigators like Beryl Bright ..."

"She's on another job," Evelyn said.

"... or Gloria Golden," Luna offered.

"Spoken for, too." Before Luna could ask, Evelyn answered, "As is Onyx Austen."

So, The Chosen One, it seemed, thought for a moment.

Luna thought for a moment. "Well, they're supposed to be forever, according to the movie. Though,

I know of something truly everlasting and more endearing."

"*God?*" Evelyn asked.

"Fraud," Luna replied.

Evelyn chuckled, "Always thinking about the job! In that case, do you remember that almost Ping-Pong ball-sized, rough red diamond found in Hawaii almost a year ago?"

Luna nodded.

"The diamond—all 110.75 fine-looking carats of it, after it was cut—was first found by an Indian cricketer named Rupert "Rupee" Sabal. He was one of the first multi-millionaires in the sport, but got hurt. Anyway, Mr. Sabal had the diamond cut and appraised. Then, Safe Pacific Property and Maritime Insurance of Honolulu insured it for $15 million."

"Did the policyholder take all the necessary steps to secure the diamond?" Luna asked.

Evelyn heaved a sigh. "Except for one," she said. "The son-of-a-gun recently toted the rock from India to Hawaii…onboard *The Shilpa*."

Luna choked on her coffee. "*You mean the ship that sank near Honolulu?!*" she coughed.

"Sure enough," Evelyn answered.

Luna recovered enough to ask if the diamond had been found yet.

"From almost 2,000 feet of water, are you kidding?" the CFO said.

"I love swimming, Evelyn, and even snagged

myself a varsity high school sports letter for it. But finding the diamond, at those depths, is a job for *The Shilpa's* owner and salvage, not me."

"Word has it that the Navy's been asked to help with salvage."

"*The U.S. Navy?!* Somebody in Safe Pacific must have some pull."

"Maybe so," Evelyn replied. "But in case they don't find the diamond at sea, we want to have our biggest, best "boots on the ground."

Luna looked down at her crossed leg and flexed her foot. "My size 10's, you mean," she concluded.

"Yep, and ready for legwork, if Mr. Sabal files a claim," Evelyn added. "We here at CPA Services handle Safe Pacific's claims, among others, and..."

"And this would sure qualify as a biggie," Luna added.

"Just so that you know, Luna, Safe Pacific doesn't suspect any wrongdoing on the part of Mr. Sabal. But, his policy has a clause that allows for investigating irregularities."

"Such as what?" Luna asked.

"Such as, why did he take the diamond onboard the ship? Why was he going to Hawaii? Why—well, I don't want to do your job for you, Luna. The point is that Safe Pacific is willing to pay you 3 percent of the value of "Pacific Splendor," as the diamond is called, for its recovery."

Luna asked, "If Pacific Splendor is still safe and sound aboard the ship, then..?"

"Then you'll have a nice vacation," Evelyn replied.

Luna wanted to be sure that it would be on the company's dime.

Evelyn gave a confirming nod. "Just bill Safe Pacific your expenses, if everything's okay."

"Three percent," Luna calculated, "should be enough to finish paying for the tractor, concession stands, and crops that I ruined when I was last here."

"Well, this job shouldn't be that difficult or destructive, Luna. There are only a few islands to check out, if it even comes to that."

"But each will have miles of beaches to browse, luaus to look into..."

Evelyn cleared her throat. "It sounds like you may need help with *focusing* your browsing and looking, Luna," she said. "So, a jewelry appraiser with Safe Pacific, Nani Nyoko, will meet you."

"This "Nani" might make for a good scout, to lead me to the diamond; or a tour guide, if the diamond's safe," Luna sized up the appraiser's value.

"Seriously, Luna, this is very important to us. This is one of the biggest shipping disasters in U.S. waters since *The Andrea Doria*. And with one of our clients right up in the middle of it..."

"I know, I know: Keep your eye on the prize, or you'll sic Dré on me again," Luna said.

"Not Dré. I know people a whole lot smarter and tougher to send," Evelyn vowed.

Luna gulped, but it wasn't coffee this time. "Right," was her nervous reply.

But Evelyn's mischievous grin put Luna at ease.

The insurance investigator finished her espresso, sat the cup and saucer on Evelyn's desk, and headed for the door. "Thanks for the job," she said. "And, to keep trouble in paradise at a minimum, I'll be in touch."

CHAPTER 5

Multi-faceted flight

Luna cancelled her flight home and scheduled another for Hawaii via Los Angeles. It wouldn't depart until the next day, leaving her in Des Moines (but not without things to do). Luna spent a couple of hours at the Jordan Creek Town Center, shopping its massive dual levels for clothing and a haircut (to make the tropical humidity bearable). On her way out, she happened by a mobile phone kiosk. One of the products being sold caught Luna's eye: An emergency cellphone.

"It's mostly for 911 calls, ma'am," the bubbly, teenaged salesgirl explained. "And, it can be left in standby mode for over two weeks without needing to be recharged. Sounds good, eh?"

Luna remembered the trouble not having a ready cellular device caused recently. An emergency phone might just come in handy, she thought. *"Sounds great!"* Luna finally told the salesgirl. "I'll take that one, Miss, the Doro 410 model." Luna also bought a few pre-paid phone cards to use with the phone, instead of getting herself bound by another cellular contract.

Once shopping was done, Luna had a quiet dinner and checked into a hotel in The Lake District. After a refreshing dip in the pool, she returned to her room, showered, set her smartphone alarm, and then caught eight hours of much-needed sleep.

Suddenly, thumping roused Luna from the beginning of a peaceful dream to the reality of more trouble. *Damn!* The insurance investigator snatched her smartphone off the nightstand and instinctively clicked its Yellow Jacket stun gun into action. Silently, Luna slipped out of bed and into her red, satin robe. She crept like a cat through the dark towards the window. A shadow flew across the drapes, and Luna hit the deck.

The "thumping" felt like oncoming footsteps. Luna crawled to the door, rose to the peephole, but couldn't see anyone outside. So carefully, she undid the chain lock, twisted the deadbolt below, and then swung the door open. Two laughing kids hurried by and into a room down the hall, unaware of the woman that almost zapped them with 60,000 volts out of fright. Luna slammed the door and struggled to sleep that night.

The next morning, Luna made the 14-minute

drive to Des Moines International Airport—this time, without trouble. She returned her car to the onsite rental company, passed TSA inspection, and prepared to board her flight. But, a severe thunderstorm warning delayed it. Storm clouds moved through and the area was pounded by wind and driving rain. But after a few hours, it was declared safe for take-off. Luna finally boarded the Central Skies Airlines737 and left for L.A.

Luna settled in and prepared to get better acquainted with Pacific Splendor. She turned on her HP Elitebook 850 laptop and pulled up a much-visited science report (authored by British geophysicist Alistair Sudhir, of Manchester University, England) on the diamond. But immediately, Luna was captured by the webpage's high resolution picture of Pacific Splendor. The brilliant round cut and ravishing, red shimmer led Luna to sigh, "What a beautiful sunset design." But when the laptop faded toward the screensaver, Luna snapped out of her daze and back into insurance investigator mode. She finished the science report and learned that red diamonds were indeed real, but rare, occurrences.

Next, Luna found the website for the lab that certified Pacific Splendor: Independent Cutting & Confirmation Enterprises (or I.C.E.). The insurance investigator couldn't find any illicit activities in their past. I.C.E. was just a small business that became an overnight player in the gem certification field (thanks to the discovery of the largest red diamond to date).

With the diamond seemingly legit, Luna switched to surfing the Web for stories on the ill-fated ship that carried it, *The Shilpa.* The big news networks still ran with reports that the ocean liner was attacked and sunk by pirates. However, the conspiracy websites' headlines warned readers to *"Remember The Maine!"* The reference was to the American warship that theorists alleged was sunk by the U.S., but blamed on the enemy, therefore provoking The Spanish-American War. They believed that something similar surrounded *The Shilpa.* But, the websites went overboard in advising readers to stock up on food, water, firearms, and underground shelter (to survive the global conflict that would surely arise from the sinking).

After Luna's laughter let up, she pulled up several mainstream news reports that detailed the growing number of bold attacks by pirates on tankers and cruise ships. At first, Luna imagined that a small pirate ship (sometimes just a raft or motorboat) attacking a large commercial vessel was like a dog chasing a car: What does it do once it catches it? In the pirates' case, they ransom the captured ship's crew or steal its cargo. After all, cruise vessels carry valuables, souvenirs, and merchandise, Luna reasoned. But the majority of such attacks were carried out by Somalis in African waters or by South Asian pirates in the Malacca Straits, not in the mid-Pacific region.

Thinking outside the box, Luna wondered if the attack was an act of terrorism. But there wasn't much to go on, regarding the politics of *The Shilpa's* passengers and crew, except that most were from India or countries nearby. Rupee Sabal was by far the most famous passenger (at least to cricket fans). But his comments to reporters over the years, including wanting to "destroy" opposing teams and "force them into submission," probably weren't threats that The World Court would consider as acts of terror.

Luna looked up public intelligence reports on the world's major and minor terrorism hot spots and perpetrators. The typical places and faces surfaced on all the sites she researched. But, Luna was surprised to find a secessionist movement afoot in Hawaii. The group that appeared on a couple of the security sites' "potential threats" sub listings was called A.L.O.H.A. (Autonomous Land of Hawaii). They hadn't *officially* claimed responsibility for the attack on *The Shilpa*—no one had so far. But, Luna noticed that they were outraged over Rupee Sabal finding Pacific Splendor. At first, they picketed and boycotted hotels, casinos, etc. Then, there were vandalisms and sit-ins that required police involvement. A.L.O.H.A. headed Luna's list of persons of interest.

After an hour, Luna took a pass on pure politics

and returned to the multi-faceted world of diamonds. But this time, she looked at ways Pacific Splendor might have been stolen. Luna read about many famous diamond heists. The Antwerp Diamond Center in Antwerp, Belgium; The Carlton Hotel in Cannes, France; and The Museon Museum of Science Heist at The Hague were just a few. But what grabbed her attention was the rise of thieves who set up seemingly legitimate jewelry investment ventures. Most were nothing more than cheap, fly-by-night fronts that cheated clients out of tens of thousands of dollars and then disappeared. But, a few of the more smooth operations still connived and thrived.

Luna looked up jewelry investors in Hawaii. She came across a company that formed less than a year before Pacific Splendor's discovery. Called Gems of the Rim Investment and owned by a Lono Kuhl, it offered up-to-the-minute stock analysis and buying advice for a variety of precious gems and jewelry. Luna couldn't find anything suspicious about Lono or the company in the online criminal databases or Better Business Bureau reports. Still, she filed him as a person of interest (if only, so far, for the athletic build, dark hair, and perfect smile portrayed by his bio page).

The policyholder, Rupee Sabal, finally drifted back into Luna's sights. With the search of the shipwreck starting up, he couldn't hope to file a claim with Safe Pacific Property and Maritime and be immediately paid. Anyway, with his millions from playing cricket, Rupee's probably enjoying Hawaii's other forms of *Pacific splendor* without worrying much about the diamond variety, Luna thought. Nevertheless, Rupee still wasn't above adding to her list of suspects.

After two solid hours of note-taking and Web-searching, Luna dozed off. A gentle tap from the stewardess woke her an hour-and-a-half later. Luna looked out the window and saw that the plane was on approach to LAX (Los Angeles International Airport). From there, Luna would change planes and begin the final 5 hour flight into the heart of the Pacific Rim: Hawaii.

CHAPTER 6

Meeting of the Minds

The Aloha State was waking up when Sky Island Air Flight 105 approached Honolulu International. Luna forgot to adjust her wristwatch to Hawaiian Standard Time and grumbled, *Five hours' time difference, eight-and-a-half hours flight—as if I didn't have enough to keep straight!* After being lassoed with the customary lei after landing, Luna got her luggage. She was about to head for the rental car company when her name was called over the PA speaker. Luna found the information desk, and waiting in front of it was an almost mirror image of herself: A tan-skinned, business-dressed lady who looked to be in her late 30's or early 40's at most. But, the lady's longer hair, shorter stature, and slightly Asian look meant Luna wasn't seeing double.

"Aloha, Luna," the business-dressed lady said, with

a welcoming smile. "I'm Nani Nyoko, jewelry appraiser with Safe Pacific Property and Maritime Insurance."

During the last leg of the trip, Luna had familiarized herself with some of the local customs. So, she approached Nani for a kiss on the cheek. Nani responded in kind. "Aloha, Ms. Nyoko," Luna replied.

"You can call me Nani," the jewelry appraiser said. "I like the blouse. Did you buy it on your stopover in L.A.?"

"In Iowa," Luna answered the question about the red, floral-patterned blouse beneath her white skirt suit jacket. "I hope it and the other clothes I bought are tropical enough."

"As one of the 50 states, we keep up with style. For business, we pretty much dress the same as you do on the Mainland: Nurses wear scrubs, lifeguards almost nothing..."

"Bummer that our investigation can't start on the beach, huh?"

"Who says it can't, Luna?" Nani supplied a wink and a grin. "Until the diamond turns up or doesn't turn up, there's not much else you can do."

"Your company wants me to hit the ground running, Nani."

"Well, you don't want to start on an empty tank, do you? Come on, let's fill 'er up with a good breakfast."

The women left the terminal and walked to the parking lot. Luna got in Nani's car and the two left the airport. "So, where's a good place to stay?" Luna asked.

"My place," Nani answered.

"No, Nani, I couldn't..."

"No, no. I insist. There aren't any kids, husband, or parents to bother. Anyway, after what I heard about your last big case, you need to save every penny. Catching bad guys with a tractor...*wow!* How did you ever get dragged into trying to "separate the wheat from the tares?"

"It's a growing field," Luna chuckled. "There's over a billion acres of land in the U.S., with over half of it used for agriculture. But, I learned that there are only about 500 employees in the whole USDA Risk Management Agency to police crop fraud. And most of them are techies who fix computers; accountants, crunching numbers in the office; and then, inspectors in the field. Five hundred people divided by over a billion acres? Do the math: RMA needs all the help it can get!"

Honolulu was awake and bustling, by the time Nani made it to the outskirts of town and her house: A bungalow that was shaded by banyan trees. The women got out, removed their shoes (a Hawaiian custom), and entered the house. Despite being filled with Polynesian antiques and a plant or two, inside was still roomy. Luna noticed a few pictures, and of particular interest was the one of a good-looking Filipino man in a fancy frame.

Nani caught Luna looking. "He's a colleague," she told her.

Luna blushed. "Sorry," she said.

"He's also fair game, if you're still hunting."

"For now, I think I better stick to "hunting" for the Pacific sort of splendor, rather than the male kind," Luna laughed.

Nani showed Luna to her room. Luna unpacked, while Nani began to cook. A half-an-hour later, the two women sat down to a breakfast of Portuguese sausages, fresh fruit, Hawaiian French toast, and guava juice.

"I've sold a few policies in my day. But, my connection with insurance has mostly been as an appraiser. First, it was property—cars, mostly. But when I was thirty-one, I found out that the engagement ring my fiancée gave me was as much of a fake as he was. Ever since then, I've been appraising jewelry," Nani told Luna.

"Trying to save some other bride from buyer's remorse?" Luna asked with a smile.

Nani sighed, "It started out as a crusade, I guess: Getting a girl to break down the sound of "I love you" and look beyond the sparkle of the ring that reels her in. But when you catch one crook, "the devil hath power to assume a pleasing shape" and cons someone new."

Luna's eyes widened. "*Shakespeare!* You and I are going to get along all right, Nani."

Nani grinned. "I had to dig deep for that one— way back to my college days. So don't get too excited," she told Luna. "But about appraising: It's just a job.

I'm not as passionate as I used to be about saving the world and everybody in it."

"Yeah, sometimes, I wish I could lay down my cross, too," Luna said. "But at 43, what else would I do?"

"What a cross to bear, though! Interesting, exciting, and, judging from the way you dress, well-paying cases," Nani replied. "Your robe…silk?"

"Satin," Luna answered the question about her red short robe. "As for being a freelance fraud investigator, it pays the bills. That crop fraud case was the exception, not the rule. Most of the cases I work are about crunching the numbers in a different way that saves the day or finding forgotten faces in boring places— far from always being "interesting and exciting.""

"Well, Luna, you could do what we're all supposed to at some point: Hunker down at home and have kids! Then, only when they're grown, try to re-establish a career—some exciting, well-paying sense of self-worth—at 60 or 70!"

Luna smiled and sipped her guava juice for the first time. The taste was different, smooth and mildly sweet. Luna liked it. She glanced out the kitchen window and also liked the view of the tropical sun, as it began asserting its golden prominence over the distant mossy peaks. "Living in such a beautiful place like Hawaii, though, probably makes it easier to think about other things—to not take the job so seriously all of the time," she said softly.

"Not this time!" Nani responded. "This case has everyone on edge. It's not every day that you run into a *red* diamond." With that, the conversation turned to the hard facts surrounding Pacific Splendor. "The price of diamonds varies and depends on things like internal flaws, color, and so on," Nani told Luna. "Replacement value of a lost diamond usually means that the insurer will pay based on the current market value at the time of the loss. But since red diamonds are some of the rarest gems in the world, Rupert Sabal opted for an agreed cash value policy and paid a year's premiums in advance. So he'll get the appraised value of Pacific Splendor as the settlement on any claim. He also took out cargo and terrorism insurance with us."

"*Hmmm,*" Luna thought aloud.

Nani looked concerned. "What?" she asked.

"Cargo *and* terrorism policies?"

"They cover perils of the seas: Fire, sinking, crew negligence, theft, and even war acts."

"Sorry. I was just curious about the need for so much extra coverage, Nani. That's all."

"Pacific Splendor is virtually priceless. No amount will truly replace its uniqueness."

Luna agreed. After finishing her sausage, she said, "I read about some different kinds of diamond heists in flight. And this Lono Kuhl guy..."

Nani nodded. "A former three-time surf champ and a runner-up other times," she said.

"Sounds like "The Big Kahuna", as they used to say in those beach movies," Luna laughed.

"Lono amassed a small fortune and then, for some reason, turned into a *gem expert*. He's one of many jewelry investment analysts, but became the most successful in the islands because of his fame. Guys like Lono try to pattern themselves after gemologists or appraisers. But, they don't often have the formal training. They don't realize that diamonds lack an historic track record to base market predictions on, Luna.

"Lono churns out what look like expert analyses. But, he usually just rakes in the investors' money with the hope that the diamonds they buy will increase in value. The thing that seems to comfort his clients the most is the facility where he stores the diamonds. It's called The Fort Rocks Repository, and investors can personally check on their holdings—even make a vacation of it.

"From all industry reports, he's doing nothing illegal, Luna. But you're right: He's worth talking to, since Rupert Sabal travelled back here to deposit Pacific Splendor at Lono's facility. And, with his knowledge of the ocean, he might be into this thing deeper than anyone thinks."

"What about this secessionist group A.L.O.H.A.?" Luna asked.

Nani's fork went down and her eyes lit up. "Now there's where I would look for suspects! They swallowed up the smaller activist groups and are now the islands' strongest separatist voice."

"We have similar groups on the Mainland. Usually, they're full of hot air. But, it sounds like yours might be hotheads."

"For years, A.L.O.H.A. was a blowhard. Then, during The Great Recession, it gained popularity. It influenced a change in law that gave greater control of mineral rights to Hawaiians and Hawaiian companies. But, it lost a bid to stop the state from setting aside a few pay-to-mine sites for tourists to pan for small amounts of olivine."

"Olivine: The green-colored crystal that looks like an emerald?" Luna asked.

Nani nodded. "It's common and only worth something, jewelry-wise, as a peridot gem."

"My grandmother had a lovely peridot ring once; that's how I knew," Luna laughed.

"Anyway, the pay-to-mine site is where Rupert Sabal found Pacific Splendor and when—well, you've read the news—protests and threats broke out. A.L.O.H.A.'s hot-and-cold activism could have boiled over into terrorism."

"So, Nani, this's not about a foreigner finding a diamond. It's about preserving power."

"You are a Native American, Luna, so you might understand A.L.O.H.A.'s position better than most. When whites forced your ancestors from their land, if they found resources there they were now theirs and not yours. A.L.O.H.A. believes that the U.S. took Hawaii by force. To them, it is still independent: The U.S. and foreigners, like Rupert Sabal, have no rights to Hawaiian assets."

"Well, how do you want to work the investigation?" Luna finally asked Nani.

"You have more all-around investigative experience than me, Luna. Like I said, until Pacific Splendor is secure, I'm basically a good hostess."

"You're more than that, Nani," Luna said. "You know the islands, the people, and how to get around. So, if you don't mind, try approaching A.L.O.H.A.'s leadership or representatives. Try not to confront them, but maybe go at it as someone who is concerned about their safety—that you're trying to get their side of the story. That might make them feel more at ease, rather than talking to an outsider like me. Also, check with the police for back-up, if you still feel threatened. I'll check with the Coast Guard; and later, Rupert Sabal and Lono Kuhl."

"Sounds good," Nani replied.

"And tastes good," Luna remarked, finishing her breakfast with a smile.

CHAPTER 7

Semper Paratus

Luna received permission to talk with the Coast Guard about the sinking of *The Shilpa*. This would have given most an excuse to prepare researching the ocean from at least the beach. But not Luna: Her first day in Honolulu was spent inland, delving into dry maritime law and history online. Nani fixed a meal of Hawaiian Gold Tilapia and mixed vegetables that brightened Luna's day, even if it was sunset when the two women enjoyed it on the backyard lawn.

Early the next morning, Nani dropped Luna by the Coast Guard 14th District Headquarters off Honolulu Harbor. Luna met with Lieutenant Sylvester Bay, the Public Affairs Officer. Bay was a tall, muscular black man, dressed in the tropical blue shirt and navy trousers uniform. After giving Luna a friendly smile and firm handshake, he opened the door to a tidy office. Bay pulled out a chair for

Luna, and then took a seat behind a desk that was decorated with the usual antique knickknacks that maritime fighting men seem to prize.

"I understand that *The Shilpa* sank in 2,000 feet of water, sir," Luna said.

"Give or take a few hundred feet," Bay replied. "She went down in the Kaiwi Channel: An area that's full of strong currents and unpredictable winds. But, the Navy has the necessary monitoring equipment and vessels to explore the wreck."

"Since the ship was attacked and sunk in our waters, sir, it's a crime scene. But it's been almost a month since the attack. Why wasn't the wreck explored immediately, before evidence was lost or contaminated?"

"Normally, Ms. Nightcrow, the salvage of civilian vessels isn't the Navy's duty. They primarily handle U.S. government-owned ships. The Coast Guard is technically responsible for patrolling and policing U.S. coastal waters. We can provide assistance to private vessels, if commercial resources aren't immediately available or adequate to the task. Otherwise, we advise and monitor the situation, but leave salvage or abandonment decisions to the owner. But, this is a special case. Do you remember that diplomatic incident back east, between the U.S. and India a year or so ago?"

Luna nodded.

"Washington wants to improve relations with a show of humanitarian aid and cooperation. Even though we responded to *The Shilpa's* distress call and used our assets to rescue the passengers and ferry them to safe haven, we delayed salvage assessments, until the Indians sent their own team of divers, oceanographers, and navy personnel. They finally arrived. So now we, along with several other federal agencies, are jointly investigating the total incident.

"But some good news is that all of the passengers survived. Unfortunately, there were two fatalities: One was the ship's engineer; the other, the pirate, who was killed by one of our helicopters from the *USCGC Armbruster*. Both sides would like to have had the pirate alive, for prosecution, but it didn't happen."

"Lieutenant, nearly all of the news reports go with the passenger and crew's testimony that a rocket-propelled grenade hit the ship and caused it to sink. And, the Coast Guard did find the spent RPG launcher, allegedly of a South Asian design. But if a rocket-propelled grenade of the small size reported hit *The Shilpa*, how could it have sunk so fast, sir?" Luna asked.

"Good question, Ms. Nightcrow," Bay responded. "It's too early to come to definite conclusions about all of this. But normally, a grenade of the quality used would probably dent, not penetrate, the hull of an ocean liner or a cruise ship. Having said that, who knows what the true strength of the hull was? If it was weak, it could have been compromised by the grenade."

"Well, she did pass her last domestic inspections, or so the Indian press reported," Luna said. "But, each cruise line's inspections probably vary, in terms of what's looked at."

Bay just nodded.

"While a single RPG probably wouldn't bring down *The Shilpa,* sir, maybe it was enough to scare the passengers and crew. The pirate could board the ship, while it was being abandoned, and rob it." But, Luna quickly developed doubts. "Then again," she said, "he'd have to know the layout of the ship. And, there was just one pirate—a lot to ask of one person."

"I put nothing past the pirate mindset," Bay replied.

"I read that federal law requires all vessels entering U.S. waters to provide you with information about their cargo, crew, etc. Were you able to determine anything about the hull integrity or discover mechanical problems through that inspection?"

"Those inspections are scheduled in advance and on a quarterly basis, Ms. Nightcrow. *The Shilpa* would have been inspected, had she reached Honolulu."

Luna pressed on. "About the pirate: Reports are that there wasn't a positive ID on him."

"There wasn't much left, after the helicopter took out his boat."

"But there was something—enough for maybe at least a racial indicator?"

"If such a determination was made, Ms. Night-crow, I wouldn't be at liberty to discuss it with you. But, I can tell you that we did identify *The Shilpa* crewman who was killed. He was the chief engineer, and it seems that he broke his neck when he jumped or fell overboard during the abandonment."

"I notice that you said "an ocean liner" or "a cruise ship." Is there a difference, sir?"

"Yes, Ms. Nightcrow. *The Shilpa* was an ocean liner: She was supposed to be more seaworthy, built to withstand the rigors of travelling from ocean to ocean. Your average cruise ship, on the other hand, is designed to travel from one regional seaport to another, or even for an outing that takes it around local waters and back to its original port in a day or two."

"So if *The Shilpa* was more of a traditional ship than a floating hotel, then why..?"

"...did she sink?" the Lieutenant finished asking. Bay reached over his desk and handed Luna a thick, accordion-style folder of information. "I gathered copies of the ship's specs, crew complement, and other vital data for you. I'll let you draw your own conclusions."

"Thank you, sir," Luna replied.

"Please remember, Ms. Nightcrow, that this is a delicate situation. We can't rush to an imme-diate conclusion that crew negligence or mechan-ical failure caused the sinking, when *The Shilpa* was obviously attacked. The implication of a biased investigation doesn't help relations."

"Likewise, sir, America doesn't want to be seen as soft on piracy. And, if simple negligence could save face, then..."

"We're exploring every scenario," Bay politely reassured Luna. "Now, Ms. Nightcrow, is there anything that I can assist you with... *regarding your search for the diamond, I mean?*"

"I didn't mean to sound like I was only interested in the sinking, sir," Luna apologized. "About "the diamond," the ship's safe hasn't been recovered yet. What priority is placed on finding it?"

"I'm unable to say, other than we're looking for it. It could have wreckage on top of it; been tossed to another part of the ship; or, heaven forbid, its contents could have been scattered on the ocean floor. Our hope is that the safe, along with other critical material, will be recovered. When that will occur? Again, I'm unable to say."

"Over 10 years ago, there was a nuclear submarine that collided with a commercial fishing ship out here. While the sunken ship wasn't brought to the surface, it was lifted to shallower depths so that most of its contents could be salvaged. Is something like that possible with *The Shilpa*, sir?" Luna asked.

"*The Shilpa's* a much larger ship, Ms. Nightcrow. But, we're still conducting total salvage feasibility assessments."

"This is one of the biggest maritime disasters to happen in U.S. waters in over 60 years," Luna said. "I read that another, the sinking of *The Andrea Doria,* also had an unusual political decision made. That was, the usual U.S. Customs check of the passengers was waived. Did that happen here?"

The Lieutenant nodded and a shrewd smile surfaced. "The Indian consulate would be a good place for specific passenger information, so that you can pursue the possibility that the diamond was smuggled out, instead of left onboard," he replied.

Luna grinned. "Forgive me, sir," she asked. "But, with a possible multi-million-dollar insurance payout depending on this, I have to consider everything that may account for a missing diamond."

"Semper Paratus, Ms. Nightcrow."

"*Sir?*" she asked.

"The Coast Guard motto: "Always ready," Bay explained. "And it's nice to know that you are, too."

CHAPTER 8

A.L.O.H.A.

Nani Nyoko's drive from Honolulu to The Autonomous Land of Hawaii (A.L.O.H.A.) headquarters took her north along Interstate H-3 towards the misty Ko'olau Mountains. She reached the town of Kane'ohe and then drove through the lush acreage of the Valley of the Temples Memorial Park. Nani's destination, in the foothills, was still a ways off. The two lane road leading up snaked through thick forest. As Nani approached a clearing, she saw the palm-thatched, triangular roofs of two tall treehouses poke through. The dual-level structures featured tropical wood balconies whose supports and railings were inlaid with images of Polynesian deities.

Nani turned off the road and into the small, gravel parking lot of the first treehouse. She parked and walked to the security gate. After buzzing the intercom, a brawny Hawaiian sentry approached.

And he wore more above the belt than below. Only the traditional *malo* (loincloth) covered his waist; and the famous *mahiole* (feathered helmet), his head. In his hand was a spear. And draped over pectorals that glistened like golden orange topaz was a crescent medallion. Nani gave the agreed-upon password (from her earlier telephone call) and the man opened the door.

Nani followed the so far silent sentry into the treehouse compound. Despite its ancient outward appearance, inside was quite modern. Off to each side of the interior's long hallway were offices, filled mostly with computers. And the few Hawaiians working inside didn't wear grass skirts, but instead dresses, slacks, and shirts. The sentry stopped and stretched out one of his massive arms. Nani followed it towards the open-air veranda. There, on the balcony, sat a white-haired, elderly woman. Wrapped in an exquisitely-tailored red and orange cape, she looked like a queen on a throne, surveying the breath-taking stretch of valley below.

The male sentry bowed to the elderly woman. "Ailani Haku, Nani Nyoko is here," he said.

The elderly woman looked over her shoulder and motioned to Nani. Nani approached and followed Ailani's command to sit in the chair next to her. The A.L.O.H.A. leader then returned to viewing the valley. "I never tire of the awesome beauty of the Autonomous Land," she sighed.

Nani tried to be diplomatic. "We at least have that in common, Ailani," she said.

"You are a local, not *kanaka maoli*: A Hawaiian," Ailani grunted.

"I can't help what I am: The daughter of a Hawaiian mother and a Japanese father," Nani remarked. "But, both helped to build and protect this island."

"It cannot be denied," Ailani admitted. "So, you have come to talk with me?"

"Yes I have, Ailani. And thank you for agreeing to talk with me. I came to ask about the sinking of *The Shilpa*."

"The ship that carried the foreigner who took the Autonomous Land's diamond," Ailani replied. "Some on Hawaii say that he actually took it from a volcano. If so, then the ship suffered the wrath of the fire goddess."

"I know of the curse on those who remove volcanic materials from the state," Nani said.

"From the "Autonomous Land of Hawaii," you should say," Ailani corrected Nani.

"Forgive me, Ailani. But then, what can you expect from a mere *local* like me?" Nani grunted.

Ailani's eyes narrowed and a knowing smile emerged. She finally turned to face her guest. "I could not have put it better," the elderly woman taunted.

Nani smiled weakly and asked, "Can we speak

openly then, instead of like a grandmother and grand-child?"

Ailani finally laughed. "All of this—the way I planned the buildings and the traditional dress of the guards—serves a purpose, you know. It is like the Native Americans' efforts on the Mainland: To preserve the past for future generations. I've seen the numbers of Hawaiians, true descendants of the Autonomous Land, lessening. We are now but 10 percent of its entire people, while the *haoles* are over half. Maybe a couple thousand of us still speak the native tongue. Prices rise, pollution infests. The future of the islands is in danger."

"So is *your* future," Nani cautioned. "The A.L.O.H.A. protests against the diamond have gained the attention of not just jewelers and their insurers, but of the government."

"The foreign powers that control the islands," Ailani sneered.

"The sinking of a vacation ship may frighten away the tourists and damage the businesses that depend on their money," Nani said. "Many people are beginning to suspect that the pirate who attacked the Indian ship was one of your members, Ailani."

"They have "suspected" many things that weren't true over the years," was how Ailani dismissed the claim.

"But many of those things were believed to be true, and became so," Nani replied.

"I can tell you that we did not destroy the foreign ship. We supported the foreigner's decision to bring the diamond back to the Autonomous Land for safe-keeping. Do you believe that will lessen your worries and those of the people who sent you?"

"Lessen, but not remove," Nani replied.

"I appreciate the honesty in your answer," Ailani told Nani. "Generations ago, to speak so boldly would be *kapu*, taboo, for a woman. It would also have been *kapu* to sit in the seat you're sitting. It was the seat of my husband and our founder."

Nani jumped up. "I didn't know that I was..."

"No, no, sit. He is gone. But his dream of separation and restoration lives. And if it is to continue we need young people like you, who sit in other seats of influence, to sit in ours."

Me, young?! Nani laughed to herself. Must be my little girl dress: Did the job, I guess! "Thanks. But, surely you have *younger* followers than me," Nani told the A.L.O.H.A. leader.

"But so few of influence," Ailani sighed. "Yes, we gained more control of our resources. And yes, we brought the diamond back to the Autonomous Land. But for all our efforts, the people give the foreign system credit for change. We are just trouble-makers. Many maids, handymen, field hands—the often oppressed—follow us. But we have fewer of wealth, celebrity, and power."

"I'm flattered that you consider me, someone

who only decides what colorful rocks are worth, as "young and powerful."

"Knowledge is a jewel itself," Ailani observed. "Tell me: What value do you place on continuing to supply A.L.O.H.A. with knowledge of the foreigners' true thoughts?"

"I'm not for sale!" Nani said firmly.

"Because you have already sold out," Ailani replied.

"If you have nothing further to add, Ailani..."

The elderly woman grabbed Nani's arm. She turned and looked her in the eye. "Those for whom you now work will sink to any depths to make money."

Nani's tone hardened. "And A.L.O.H.A. may have sank a ship and its future," she warned.

"Be careful, as you look for the diamond, Nani Nyoko."

"Are you afraid of what I might dig up, Ailani?"

Ailani shook her head "no." Her grip on Nani's arm loosened. "What you have dug is a hole for yourself, I am afraid."

Nani pulled away from the elderly woman. She turned and mockingly bid Ailani, *"Aloha."* Nani left the balcony and was escorted by the brawny Hawaiian sentry to the outside gate. He opened it and Nani stepped through. The sentry then watched Nani get in her car and drive away.

CHAPTER 9

Divide and Conquer

Nani arrived at Honolulu Harbor around noon to pick up Luna. "I don't know whether to laugh or cry, Luna," the jewelry appraiser huffed.

"That bad, huh?" Luna asked.

"It was like being in an amusement park. But, the only *amusement* was in all the historical flaws! First, the guards are dressed more like noblemen than true Hawaiian warriors of ancient times. Then A.L.O.H.A.'s latest leader, an elderly woman named Ailani Haku, ranted about returning to the past. But, the headquarters are modern, million-dollar offices— monuments to Ailani's architectural ego. Finally, The Godmother tries to bribe *and* threaten me!"

"The Godmother"…*priceless!*" When her laughter stopped, Luna asked, "Did they deny involvement in the attack?"

"Obviously they did."

"Given what you saw, you still believe they're *really* capable of the sinking?"

"Yes, Luna!" It became quiet for a couple of minutes. Nani cooled off and said, "I'm sorry for yelling, Luna. Who knows? It could have all been a put-on, the wolf in sheep's clothes routine. Okay, cheer me up with what you got from the Coast Guard."

"The Indians are working with the feds and the military on salvaging *The Shilpa's* safe. But, it's in about 2,000 feet of water. There's no telling when it will be raised. But maybe the biggest thing is that the pirate boat's fire power wasn't sufficient to sink that ship."

"Is that what the Coast Guard thinks?" Nani asked.

"They think I should "draw my own conclusions," and gave me the ship's design and crew information. From what I've browsed so far, I think the ship was too old to be used as an ocean liner. It may have sunk due to mechanical wear and tear or sloppy maintenance."

Nani asked, "So, they're ruling out the pirate attack?"

"It's all about politics. "They" still have everything on the table, until both sides agree to remove something," Luna said. "For me, it's about trying to stay busy and build a case and some leads. The ship stored Pacific Splendor; that's my only connection to the incident. But trying to sink a ship with just one man and one rocket seems crazy to me."

"Exactly something those A.L.O.H.A. loons might do: Think that they can go from protests to military action in just a few months," Nani reasoned. "Did you happen to ask about the pirate? Like whether they found out who he was?"

"Probably Hawaiian, from the public relations officer's dodging the question of whether the remains were at least racially identified," Luna answered. "He was too quick to tell me about the Indian engineer's identity and cause of death, meaning..."

"They're going to cover up that a radical Hawaiian may be responsible and blame it all on the Indians," Nani concluded.

"Well, not me," Luna assured her. "A.L.O.H.A. is still on my sonar."

"All right, Luna, what's next?"

"Did you know that in India, Nani, 122 different languages are spoken?"

"I do now," Nani replied. "Do you speak one of them?"

"We both do: English," Luna answered.

"But, how many of the passengers of *The Shilpa* do?"

"That's what I want you to find out. The U.S. Customs inspection was waived because of a fairly recent diplomatic spat between India and America. If Pacific Splendor isn't in the safe, it must be because someone smuggled it off the ship during the attack. The list of ship's passengers and crew is in the Coast Guard files. You know Honolulu; so, find out where everyone is staying. We may need to talk to several of them, especially crew members."

"I don't know about the crew, Luna. Are they going to rat out unsafe work conditions, if they hope to work for the cruise line again?"

"Remember that it's information about Pacific Splendor we're looking for, Nani. The cruise company's labor practices are their own business, unless they relate to our case."

"Most of the passengers have probably already returned to India, too," Nani added.

"Yeah, the disaster ruins the vacation," Luna said. "But some passengers pass on travel insurance and get stuck."

"But, it's closing in on three weeks since the attack," Nani replied. "I've been around insurance enough to know that by now, emergency claims to the cruise line will probably start to pay for at least the transportation home for stranded passengers."

"I'm willing to bet that with the international search for *The Shilpa's* safe underway, many passengers are staying to see what turns up," Luna said.

"We're probably going to need an interpreter," Nani added. "If the Indian consulate can't provide one, I'll check the local colleges for professors or students who might be willing to help." Nani eyed

Luna curiously. "So while I'm doing all that, Luna, what will you be up to?"

Luna grinned. "Brushing up on my cricket," she answered. "Specifically, my attacking shot."

CHAPTER 10

A Dangerous Drink

Luna found out where Rupee Sabal was staying and gave him a call. The cricketer agreed to meet her for drinks. The location he gave led Luna to unpack something that she hoped would persuade Rupee to do more than just drink.

Late the next day, a fleet of Indian and American ships was still anchored offshore. The crews were too busy combing the murky ocean bottoms to notice the spectacular bright-red sunset that spilled from above. Luna didn't notice it much either. The only lights she saw were the illuminated, GPS-generated street designs that crisscrossed her smartphone screen. And the only sound was that of the automated guidance system (customized for a mellow, manly voice). But as the sky darkened, the glow from downtown Honolulu was enough to guide Luna in. As the bumper-to-bumper traffic and high-rises increased, she wondered if she was still in paradise.

Luna pulled Nani's Mitsubishi Mirage into the driveway of the Waikiki Hilton. Instantly, a young valet appeared from the posh surroundings to greet her. Luna handed him the car keys; then, a tip; and finally, headed for the hotel entrance. She stopped at the front desk and asked where the Luau Lounge was. Luna found the interior, courtyard-styled bar and made a spectacular entrance. Sweeping through in a sleeveless, coral satin dress and matching pumps, she turned the heads of the male patrons and the stomachs of their comparatively dressed-down female companions.

Luna parked her handbag on the bar and took a seat. Before the bartender could get to her, someone else did. "Namaste," Luna heard a light, but still masculine, voice say. She turned almost directly into a lean, swarthy man's intent look. His thick, moussed hair was as black as his tuxedo and his gray eyes danced with delight. "You must be the lovely Luna Nightcrow," the man said.

"*Namaste?*" Luna asked.

"In Hindi, it means "I bow to the godly in you." Or, put simply, it means "hello" or "good-bye," and is a relief from always hearing "aloha."

"So, you are the dashing cricketer Rupert Sabal.

I'm sorry that I didn't recognize you sooner, but the goatee…"

"A benefit of not playing the game is to look how you would like, not how you must," Rupee answered.

Luna extended her hand. In it was her business card.

Rupee took the card; then, Luna's empty hand. He raised it to his lips. The kiss Luna felt was warm and inviting. The cricketer then looked up and into the insurance investigator's dark brown eyes; and she, into his gray gaze. "My friends call me "Rupee." So, please, call me Rupee."

"But we barely know each other," Luna laughed.

Rupee looked at the business card. "You are the American Indian insurance investigator; and I, an Indian sportsman. Two Indians, of a sort: Is that not something to build a relationship upon?"

"A *friendship*, you mean?" Luna asked guardedly.

"Yes, yes," Rupee chuckled, "so many expressions to learn in English!" He finally took a seat beside the insurance investigator. "What shall you have? It's my treat."

The bartender appeared. Luna ordered a Maui Breeze (a pink, guava juice-based cocktail); and Rupee, a Bombay Sapphire. "So, that's why they call you "Rupee": You have so many of them to spend," Luna guessed.

"Yes, I have money," Rupee replied, "if only enough to buy you a drink."

"A man who would offer a woman everything—wow, I'm impressed!"

"I would offer you even the moon, but you already have its beauty. Is that not why they call you "Luna?"

"I think it's because I'm a smart bird who works her butt off and rarely gets a good night's sleep. Because, I'm all yours: Day or night, but only if the price is right," was Luna's reply.

Rupee laughed, "In India, to tell a woman that she is more beautiful than the moon is considered an honor." Then he sighed. "Alas, we are not in India. But, I believe that we shall talk of Indian matters, namely the sinking of a certain passenger ship and its cargo, yes?"

"Yes," the insurance investigator agreed. The drinks arrived and Rupee paid the bartender. "But first, Rupee, I want to get to know more about you."

"What more is there to know that you haven't already learned from the news, Luna? I am just a cricketer, whose career is probably over."

"I wouldn't say that," Luna argued. "You're only 38 years old."

"I have played since the age of 18. I feel like an old man, against today's faster players."

"What about those 2 First-Class hundreds you scored in the Pro Indian League?"

"You forgot to mention the one timed out against me; the only one the League has seen."

"So what if you weren't ready to play within three minutes of the last batter being out? Who's perfect, Rupee?"

"You are a kind woman, Luna, as well as a lovely one."

Luna's fingers frolicked along the rim of her drink, before she lifted it to her lips. After a nip, she asked, "How did you get hurt, Rupee?"

"I played too hard. I was an all-rounder: An aggressive bowler and batsman who played each inning as if it were my last. At first, I thought my injury was just not cricket."

Luna was confused. "Not *cricket-related*, you mean?" she asked.

"Oh, no, I mean the saying "not cricket." You might say "not fair," Rupee explained. "But, I came to learn that when the match is done there is no true consequence; it is just a game. Some new player shall win the crowd's praise or break your records. Everyone in cricket learns that he has but a short span, and that he must make plans for another life. So, I dreamed of achieving something lasting, something to be truly remembered for."

"Is that why you came to Hawaii?" Luna asked.

Rupee nodded. "I read tales of hidden treasures to be found in the islands of the Pacific. So, after a match in Australia, I came here to search. I found a diamond and gave it the name Pacific Splendor. It was a gift not only for me, but for all of Hawaii.

After I found it and had it cut and appraised, I felt ashamed for keeping it far away in Mumbai. So, I returned here: To have it studied and then stored by some of Hawaii's own people. But now, the diamond is lost at sea probably."

Luna planted her chin on her palm. Her fingers thrummed her cheek thoughtfully. "You seem so certain of that," was the insurance investigator's conclusion.

Rupee took a sip of Bombay Sapphire. "Your job is to question my certainty?" he asked, sitting the martini glass aside.

Luna smiled. "Yes, that's part of my job. Until your government and ours recover the ship's safe and—well, I have to worry about Pacific Splendor's whereabouts."

Rupee smiled. "To keep you from worrying so, I shall hope it is still in the ship's safe."

"Why wouldn't it be, Rupee?"

"Under so much water, would not the pressure destroy the safe and scatter its contents?"

"I've seen some pretty strong safes that can withstand a lot of abuse," Luna replied.

"The pirate boat..." Rupee began to say. With that, Luna's ears perked up. "What if the pirate had friends in Hawaii who helped him to sink *Shilpa*, Luna?"

"Pirates usually don't want to sink a ship, but rob it instead."

"What if they are not pirates, but terrorists?"

"Now you're starting to sound like a friend of mine, Rupee!"

"Is this "friend" also an insurance investigator?"

"Sort of," Luna replied.

"Sort of, for instance, a *male* investigator?"

"No," Luna answered firmly. "And *no*, there aren't any other males…"

"Forgive me, Luna, I only meant that you may need a male to protect you…" Rupee suddenly stopped and looked around suspiciously. "Perhaps it is no longer safe to talk here."

Luna cast an eye over the lounge and noticed a hefty, Hawaiian-looking man standing in the far corner behind them. He wore a tuxedo and was probably just checking out Rupee's. But the scowl that he shot at them meant that he either didn't like Rupee's taste in tux or his taste in women. *This might turn out to be a dangerous drink!* Luna worried. But looking back at Rupee, she saw that he was still visibly shaken. I've got to be the strong one, Luna decided. So, she dragged a red fingernail up and down the back of Rupee's hand. "Where do you suggest we talk, if not here?"

Rupee's eyes widened. "Well, this is a hotel; so, it does have rooms," he suggested.

Luna's eyebrow cocked curiously. "Where's yours, Rupee?" she asked softly.

A smile returned to Rupee's face and he answered, "It's a big one, Luna, way up high."

Just what a girl likes to hear! Luna thought. "Will you please get the elevator, Rupee?"

Once Luna saw Rupee leave, she then signaled for the bartender. "Yes, ma'am?" he asked.

Luna dug through her handbag. "That guy with the tux in the corner: Is he the bouncer or hotel security?" she muttered.

The bartender took a look. "No and no," he answered. Then, the young man took a look at Luna. It was a much longer look than he gave the hefty man. "That's a nice dress," he told her.

Luna took out two $20 bills and slapped them on the bar. "Buy yourself a dress; the guy, a drink; and me, some time," she told the bartender.

The hefty man in the tux saw Luna leaving. He unfolded his big arms and moved quickly for the exit too. The bartender called out, *"Hey, brah,"* and the hefty man stopped. The young man waved him over and held out a coconut shell with a pink umbrella in it. "On the house," he announced.

"On you!" the hefty man growled. He slapped the tropical drink out of the bartender's hand and continued pursuit.

Luna hiked her dress and hurried down the hall, looking for Rupee. But she found only doors to suites, instead. *Where the hell is he?!* Luna thought. She stopped for a moment and unfastened her handbag. Before she could pull out her smartphone, the insurance investigator heard her name being called.

"LUNA!" When she stopped and looked around the corner, on the other side she saw a smiling Rupee wave from down the hall. "I have the elevator," he announced.

Luna looked back up the hall and saw that the hefty man had entered. And when he saw Luna, he sped up. Luna reached into her handbag, pulled out her Doro 410 emergency cellphone, and turned it sideways. *"Back off!"* she shouted, aiming it directly at the hefty man.

The hefty man was still a good distance away, but stopped and raised his hands in the air. *It worked!* Luna thought. He thinks it's a pocket pistol!

Slowly, Luna backed her way down the hall. But she noticed the hefty man inching forward. Without a warning shot to fire, the trick was wearing off. So Luna suddenly turned the corner and raced down the hall for the elevator. She could hear the hefty man closing in. Luna finally got to the elevator and pushed Rupee inside. She stumbled, but it was into his arms.

"A good catch, yes?" Rupee asked.

Luna smiled. "I told you that your career wasn't over yet," she remarked.

Outside, the doors closed on the glare of a man who missed more than just the elevator.

CHAPTER 11

All Work

Luna and Rupee engaged in an hour's worth of hotel elevator and stairwell hide-and-seek and seemed to escape their hefty hunter. They finally arrived at the top floor and stepped into a beautiful, cream-colored hallway. But to Luna, the only nice thing about it was that it was empty. With her Yellow Jacket smartphone stun gun in hand, she hurried Rupee down the hall. They arrived at his suite, where the cricketer took an electronic card from his jacket and inserted it into the lock. The door barely opened to a dark crack when Luna rushed through. *"Ladies first!"* was her excuse for being hasty.

Luna flipped on the lights. Ignoring the luxurious decor, she pulled open every door: To the bathroom; then, the closet; next, the bedroom; and finally, to the balcony. *No one!* Luna sighed. She unfastened her handbag, stashed her smartphone inside, and tossed it into the bedroom. The handbag must have travelled a mile, before it landed on the nearest double bed!

Luna returned to the balcony. Instantly, her shoulders and guard dropped, both enraptured by the relaxing rush of evening breeze gusting off the Pacific. Suddenly, Luna felt something heavier than the cool air fall upon her shoulder. She jumped and spun around, but only saw Rupee. He raised both hands in the air, stepped back into the bedroom, and chuckled, *"I surrender!"*

"Sorry, Rupee," Luna apologized.

"It is I who should be sorry, for disturbing you," he replied.

Luna motioned for the cricketer to come outside. He hesitated, but then smiled and stepped through. Luna returned to concentrating on the invigorating view.

"I wish that I could look out at the night as easily as you, Luna. Perhaps it is easy for you because you are of the moon. But, I can't bear to look because the lights of the buildings and the cars remind me of that diamond's sparkle."

Luna turned around. "You were going to tell me more about "that diamond," remember?" she reminded Rupee.

"Yes, of course," he replied. "I could not say more in the bar. Who knows if they might have agents there?"

"The pirate's friends, you mean?"

"No, the terrorists who want Hawaii to leave

your country. They call themselves A.L.O.H.A., after the saying, and could be everywhere. I believe they attacked *Shilpa*. If one of them can't have the diamond, then no one can. Or, perhaps they attacked *Shilpa* to get the diamond, sell it, and then use the money to buy weapons for their cause. I thought that to bring the diamond back for all Hawaiians to see would be good. But, it has caused more trouble, Luna."

Luna sighed, "Maybe it has. Maybe…"

Before Luna could finish, Rupee raised a finger. She eased off her anxiety, when Rupee reached out and delicately traced an invisible line that felt like lust along one of her bare shoulders. The cricketer asked gently, "Since we are safe now, Luna, must we continue to talk only of upsetting things?"

"Maybe we shouldn't," she answered.

"Talk only of the diamond, you mean?"

Luna nodded. Then, she crossed the line Rupee drew, mimicking his finger play with a stroke of his goatee. "After all, you know what they say…?"

Rupee cut in again; this time, to reach for the soft part of Luna's arms. He captured them and guided her body towards his. Luna slowly shaped a little smile. When it became full, it lit up Rupee's night with absolute delight. And at last, they kissed— softly, at first. But when Rupee let go, Luna looped her arms around his neck and returned for more. The couple embraced and backed into the bedroom, where they plunged into passion. Rupee's caresses explored Luna's curves and crevasses. And she rolled her fingers through the dark waves of Rupee's thick hair. Their lips unlocked, but their hold remained firmly in place.

Suddenly, Luna's eyes blinked open and returned to work. They scanned the bedroom over Rupee's shoulder. Again, Luna saw no one else. But she did notice something she didn't see before: On the floor, near the corner of one of the beds, was what looked like a sports bag.

"Luna?" Rupee breathed.

Luna had to return to form. *"Yes, Rupee?"* her husky voice moaned, matching his intensity.

"What do they say?"

"What does who say?" Luna then remembered. "Oh, yes: "All work and no play make Jill a dull girl.""

"I would agree," Rupee whispered, as he nibbled Luna's earlobe.

The insurance investigator then pushed him away. *"Wonderful!"* she exclaimed, preserving a smile. "I hoped you'd agree!"

Rupee was clearly confused. *"Agree?!* To what, Luna?" he stammered.

"To teach me how to improve my cricket swing, of course," Luna answered.

"What gave you such an idea?" Rupee asked.

"That bag beside your bed," Luna pointed out. "It looks like a sports bag. You must have saved it from your ship."

"Certainly, I did. But, it is empty. My equipment, alas, sank with *Shilpa*," Rupee groaned. "The carrying case is but a keepsake."

"I'm so sorry, Rupee. You seem upset. Maybe this isn't a good time to learn cricket. I-I tend to come on a bit too strong sometimes," Luna apologized.

Rupee couldn't let the chance for romance get away. "Oh, no: I'm not upset, Luna!" he insisted "Please, stay. I shall find something similar to a bat!"

Rupee left the bedroom. *Perfect!* Luna hurried for her handbag. She grabbed it and rummaged through it. She could hear the clatter from Rupee pulling out something in the kitchenette. With him distracted, Luna found a fingernail file. She rushed to the sports bag, unzipped it, and sliced a small section from the inside lining. The insurance investigator stood.

"Ah-ha!" Rupee announced moments later. With a long-handled pot in hand, he victoriously re-entered the bedroom. But, it was an empty bedroom. Luna was nowhere in sight. *"Luna?"* Rupee called.

Luna had long since left and was now halfway down the hallway. In her hand wasn't the emergency phone as before, but now the Yellow Jacket stun gun-sheathed smartphone (with her thumb poised to pop it into action at the first sign of trouble). But there was none; the rest of the way to the elevator posed no threat. Luna rode down and went to the front desk. A new valet escorted her to her car. Luna tipped him and climbed in. Before firing up the GPS (for the ride to Nani's) the insurance investigator let out a long sigh of relief. *What a night!* She just hoped that Rupee would be all right.

As Luna pulled out of the hotel parking lot, someone rose from the shadows of a parked car. It was the hefty man. He raised a smartphone. And instead of a scowl, his face was now filled with delight at the sight of a license plate number plastered across the illuminated screen. He may have missed Luna before, but he had her now. And so would the party he forwarded the picture to.

CHAPTER 12

Discovery

A black motorcycle buzzed by and then the sound of kids down the street playing while awaiting the school bus greeted Nani Nyoko, as she stepped outside for the newspaper. She came inside to the sight of Luna trudging into the kitchen. "Aloha," Nani called, shutting the front door.

Luna yawned and waved in Nani's general direction. She plopped down at the table.

"I didn't hear you come in last night. So, did your red satin dress do the trick?" Nani asked.

Luna poured herself some Kona and only came to life after the first few sips. *"Coral dress, red satin robe,"* she gently corrected Nani's fashion faux pas. "Yeah, my dress got the women's blood pressures up and raised the guys'—well, let's just say that it made quite the impression."

"Did it impress the *right* guy?"

"Rupee will be wedded to your company, 'til a

claim do you part. Oh, that reminds me..." Luna reached into the pocket of her red satin short robe and pulled out a plastic bag. It contained a black strip. "Can you have Safe Pacific run an analysis of this for traces of diamond particles?"

Nani chuckled, "That's not quite how it works, Luna, but sure. What is it, by the way?"

"It's a piece of Rupee's cricket bag. He is a possible suspect. I mean, he's convinced that his career is over with. And he carries an empty cricket bag with him off the ship as "a keepsake?"

"But, Luna, he's also a millionaire—a good-looking one, at that," Nani reminded her. "What are 15 million extra bucks from faking a diamond loss worth to him? Besides, even if the analysis tests positive, who's to say that Rupert didn't carry Pacific Splendor in the bag while going onboard the ship in India and while transferring it to the ship's safe?"

"Yeah, I know," Luna admitted to all of it. "But still: He saves the bag, but forgot to pack his cricket gear? The bag was empty when I checked it. I could have paid a maid or a bellhop to snoop around his suite. But so far, this's just a life-sized version of *Clue* we're playing."

Nani's jaw dropped. *"You got this from his hotel room?!"*

Luna was only able to wink, as a sip of coffee concealed what would have been a sinful smile. But she finally explained, "A Hawaiian-looking man—a bodybuilding type—watched us at the bar and then chased us onto the elevator. That's how I ended up in Rupee's room. It may build a case for your A.L.O.H.A. anxiety—a worry that, you'll be happy to know, Rupee shares too."

"Now when you say "Hawaiian-looking," Luna, I must caution you," Nani advised. "Hawaiian" here, more and more, means someone who is a Pacific Islander by race. Someone born here or who lives here, but isn't Hawaiian, is a "local." Since I'm the product of a mixed marriage I am *hapa*, or part, and usually called a local. To A.L.O.H.A. types, you would be a *haole,* or foreigner. So, this bad guy looked more like what: A Hawaiian, a local of another race, or *haole*?"

The smell of breakfast being served sharpened Luna's senses a bit. "I'd say more Pacific Islander, but I can't be 100 percent sure," she responded. After a few bites of spam and rice and copious con-sumptions of Kona, Luna switched topics. "So, did you find an interpreter?"

"The consulate will supply one," Nani said. "Also, Safe Pacific is prepared to offer a reward, if…"

The ringtone of a smartphone interrupted the conversation. It was Luna's. She plucked the phone from the pocket of her robe. "Hello?" the insurance investigator answered.

"Good morning, Ms. Nightcrow," the male voice beamed. "Gotten used to the time difference yet?"

"Good afternoon, Lieutenant Bay. Does that answer your question?"

"I'm from Baltimore, originally. So I can relate," Bay laughed. "As a kid, the only thing I wanted to travel a long distance through the air was a perfectly-thrown, 50-yard pass from my hands into John Mackey's for the Colts." Bay then got down to business. "The reason I called is because late last night, a mini-sub located *The Shilpa's* safe. It just broke in most of the media."

"That's great news!" Then, Luna asked, "But whose sub found it, theirs or ours?"

"Ours: It was *The Discovery*, appropriately enough!" Bay proudly announced. "With the passengers and crew accounted for, Washington's returned to the normal Customs routine: That means a full Hazmat inspection for chemical, biological, or nuclear threats. The Indians are tickled pink to get their hands on the safe and are willing to play ball. The cruise line released the combination to Customs and the decontamination will be videotaped. By the way, I got you credentials for the press conference. We'll ceremonially re-open the safe and take questions."

"I also have an investigator from Safe Pacific Property and Maritime, the diamond's insurer, working with me. Is it too late to get credentials for her, too?"

"That shouldn't be a problem, Ms. Nightcrow."

"About what time will they open the safe?"

"While *The Discovery* found the safe, raising it is another matter. Last estimates as to the time of recovery were about 5 p.m. local time. The press conference will be at about 7 or 8 pm."

"I'll set my smartphone, for Hawaiian time, and be there," Luna said.

Bay chuckled, "Good day, Ms. Nightcrow."

"Thanks again and good-bye, Lieutenant." Luna looked across the table. "You heard?"

"Yes. That's wonderful," Nani replied. "But, a word of caution..."

Luna's eyes lit up. *"What?"* she asked.

"Don't wear the satin dress this time, Miss Scarlet."

"Is that a *clue* that I should wear the red satin robe, instead?" Luna asked.

Both women broke into laughter.

CHAPTER 13

Behind the Door

Luna and Nani left early for the press conference. They stopped by 14th District Headquarters and picked up the press credentials. Then, they
headed for the U.S. Navy's recently-built special
decontamination facilities near the Pearl Harbor
Memorial. Luna didn't get to see the sights along
the way, as she sat glued to her smartphone for live
streaming coverage of the raising of the safe. She
surfed from one news site to the next, looking for
any clues as to whether the safe was breached. She
got mostly commentary and computer analyses of
the salvage. When live coverage of the safe being
raised was finally shown, Luna still couldn't tell
what was inside.

Nani pulled into the decontamination facility
parking lot. Inside, Luna and she showed their credentials, passed metal detection, and were finally
directed to the designated press conference site.

The heat from everyone's excitement and nervousness overpowered the air-conditioning. But Nani seemed to be enjoying the event, as she mingled with reporters from around the world and with the ocean line reps, feds, and military dignitaries. Luna, on the other hand, took an early seat and sweated.

About an hour later, the room's large double doors opened. And first to enter was a cart that carried a five-foot tall, re-enforced titanium box with a punch key combination lock on its door. It was pushed to the front. The crush of cameras created a field of fluid blue flashes that gave the full effect of the safe being raised again. Luna could only get a passing glimpse of the safe's outer condition. From that limited view, it looked remarkably preserved (for being pressed upon for weeks by over a thousand feet of sea water).

"Ladies and gentlemen, may I please have your attention?" a familiar-sounding voice asked. It took a few minutes for the audience to comply. When it did, Luna saw Lieutenant Bay at the podium and naval officers and suited executives from India and the U.S. sitting on either side. "Thank you for your patience and understanding in this matter," he began again. "Let me first say that, on behalf of the United States Coast Guard 14th District, Honolulu, we are grateful for the support of the Indian Navy and the help of oceanographers and divers from the Indian Oceanographic Agency. We also applaud the success of the U.S. Navy's Deep Sea Submersible Team. Without the joint efforts of our two nations, the recovery of phase of *The Shilpa* would have taken a great deal longer to achieve."

Bay then thanked several other key military and civilian personnel before continuing.

"I would like to also say that this is just the beginning of our joint investigation into *The Shilpa* Incident. Tonight's proceedings are designed to first reveal the contents of the safe that was recovered and then answer questions pertaining to what was or wasn't found. The Coast Guard and the Indian and United States Navies would like to ask that questions pertaining to other aspects of *The Shilpa* Incident please be held for future conferences. With that said, I will turn the proceedings over to The Honorable Mr. Vijay Varun, President of Sagar Excursions."

Bay shook the hand of a well-dressed Indian executive who approached the podium. After another long speech, Varun finally announced the ceremonial opening of the safe. Two naval officers (one American and one Indian) approached. The room was again awash in a flickering flood of blue flashbulb bursts. Luna's hands shook, as one officer opened the heavy door. The other began to remove objects and hold them up in the air. Souvenirs, travelers' checks, and what looked like certificates (maybe for stocks and bonds) emerged. Where's Pacific Splendor? Luna thought. One last item was retrieved: A black metal box. Luna recognized it as the type used in bank vaults. *This had to be it!* Everyone stood, as the Indian officer opened the box. Luna's central seating caused her to miss what happened next.

Everything was carefully laid out on the tables in front of the podium. Varun began taking questions from the press. The first was about the black metal box's contents. Varun adjusted the microphone and answered, in several languages, "It is empty." A collective gasp seized the crowd. Varun calmed everyone and braced himself for the onslaught of questions about the whereabouts of Pacific Splendor.

Luna was relieved to finally know what happened. Unlike most of the crowd, she was prepared for the possibility that the diamond wouldn't show up. Her preliminary legwork gave her a leg up on the media and treasure hunters. And now, it was time to get on with the task of recovering Pacific Splendor before they did.

CHAPTER 14

Game on

With Pacific Splendor officially missing, it was game on for Luna and Nani. So instead of continuing to share her host's car, the next day Luna rented one: A rather modest, gray Ford Fusion SE that would be perfect for any surveillance duty that might come about. She was on the final page of digital paperwork when her smartphone rang.

"Hello?" Luna answered.

"Good afternoon, Luna."

"*Rupee!* It's good to hear from you. Are you okay?" Luna asked.

"I would be better, if I could have remained at the Waikiki Hilton and showed you some cricket moves," he sighed.

Luna finished signing the paperwork and handed the tablet back to the rental car rep. "You're no longer at the hotel, Rupee?"

"For my safety, I have moved."

"*Good!* But don't tell me where."

"Then how shall you ever find me, Luna?"

Luna got into her car. "Pacific Splendor, remember?" she said.

That made Rupee's tone pick up. *"Ah, yes!* I saw the news last night. If the diamond cannot be found, then I shall call you and we can arrange a meeting for the immediate acceptance of my claim for payment."

Luna knew it would come to that. "Rupee, you do understand that before the insurance company will pay any claim on Pacific Splendor, they will want to conduct a full investigation into the circumstances of its disappearance?" she asked.

"Yes, I understand, Luna. But, I told you that I believe it was stolen by *those people* we talked of, remember?"

"And I'm investigating them."

"Are the police investigating them, too?"

"They have before. But right now, Rupee, this is an insurance matter."

"They are dangerous people, Luna. How can you hope to arrest them alone?"

"I'm not going it "alone," Luna assured Rupee. "By the way, do you mind if I ask you a few more questions about Pacific Splendor?"

"Please do, Luna," Rupee replied.

"Why choose Independent Cutting & Confirmation Enterprises to certify the diamond?"

"I know that they are small. But, when compared to some of the more famous gem labs' scandals, their flawless reputation and independence were why I chose them. Is that bad, Luna?"

"It makes sense," she replied. "About the safe: It wasn't damaged when it was raised and, when opened, its contents were in perfect condition. You did put Pacific Splendor in the safe upon boarding *The Shilpa* and leave it there throughout the trip?"

"Yes, of course, Luna."

"You also planned to have the jewelry investment CEO Lono Kuhl hold Pacific Splendor. Did you two ever meet or talk at length before *The Shilpa* sank?"

"We never met personally. But, we did talk over the phone about safeguarding the diamond. We are both former sportsmen; so, we also exchanged stories of the rigors of competition and..." There was a brief silence. "Luna," Rupee then asked, "is it possible that Lono, a Hawaiian, could be involved in all of this? I believe he does have A.L.O.H.A.'s endorsement."

"I don't know. But, do you see why my investigation might take a while to complete?"

"I shall give you whatever time you need to investigate, Luna," Rupee said. "I believe you to be a fair woman and one also capable of determining the diamond's fate. I would offer to assist you, but I have other affairs to attend to in Honolulu. One of them is ensuring my safety."

"Thank you, Rupee," Luna replied. "I would ask for your help, but we might not be able to concentrate on work after—well, you do remember, don't you?"

"All play and no work would, in this matter, make Jill unable to find Pacific Splendor," Rupee laughed. "Take care."

"Stay safe and in touch, Rupee," Luna replied. The line dropped off, but Luna decided to make a call to the one man whom she was very suspicious of from the start, Lono Kuhl.

Luna found the number to Gems of the Rim Investment. The receptionist said Lono was unavailable, but connected Luna to his voicemail (where she left a message asking to talk about Pacific Splendor). Luna then found the firm's website on her smartphone. The insurance investigator noticed that Lono was scheduled to host a Gems of the Rim seminar the next evening.

Luna started the car and finally returned to Nani's house. When she walked in, she saw that Nani had a visitor: A cherubic, dark-skinned young woman, wrapped in a colorful sari. Before Nani could introduce her, the visitor eagerly introduced herself. "I am Narmata Buddhiman, Chief Interpreter for the Indian Consulate," she said, with a big smile and eyes racing with excitement behind her glasses. "I am so happy to assist you. When will questioning begin?"

"Uh, Nani will handle "questioning" the passengers and crew, Ms. Buddhiman," Luna said. "I just need for you to translate what she asks and what they say as accurately as possible, okay?"

"Oh, I will! You needn't worry, Luna. Forgive my excitement, but I have followed the story about the diamond. It is so beautiful, and it would be such an honor to help recover it."

"Yes, recovering it would be wonderful. May I talk privately with Nani, please?"

"I do not mind, Luna," Narmata replied. She left the living room for the backyard.

"She really is a nice girl," Nani commented.

"Yeah, but a little too pumped up," Luna said.

"I know how she feels," Nani laughed. "We've been chatting about how our jobs keep us mostly cooped up in an office all day. So, this case is a nice little adventure."

"I got a call from Rupee," Luna said.

"Don't tell me: He's going to file his claim," Nani groaned.

"Just the opposite," Luna answered. "He told me to take my time investigating. I guess that satin dress really did do the trick."

"Having millions of dollars takes the load off, too," Nani laughed. "Well, there are 95 passengers and the crew of *The Shilpa* left in Hawaii. When do you want to start asking them for interviews?"

"You and Narmata start ASAP," the insurance investigator said. "I need to track down a player in this that I haven't talked to."

CHAPTER 15

Mr. Kuhl

Luna didn't receive a return call from Lono Kuhl. So, the next afternoon, she drove to his seminar. Luna paid the $50 entrance fee and browsed the sales tables outside the Marriott Suites conference room. She collected some free pamphlets and found a seat near the front inside. The lights gradually dimmed and at 6 p.m., Lono Kuhl pranced out. The picture Luna saw of him in-flight didn't do him justice. Besides the big man on campus physique, the 40-year old possessed an infectious sense of humor that showed through his white blazer and loud Aloha shirt.

Lono clowned around but eventually got down to an effective Power Point presentation about the jewelry industry. And at 8 p.m., he left the floor to thunderous applause. Outside, Lono was engulfed in a sea of young and old well-wishers and the product tables swelled with buyers. Luna waited patiently for the crowd to thin. Then, the insurance investigator walked up.

"Mr. Kuhl?" Luna asked.

Lono turned around. He looked Luna up and down. A smile indicated that he like what he saw. "Well, aloha, Miss...?"

"Nightcrow, Luna Nightcrow. I'm representing Safe Pacific Property and Maritime Insurance, Honolulu. Can we please talk?"

Lono's smile shriveled. "I had *Pacific splendor* as a surfer, and should have had it now as a broker. In case that wasn't clear, I didn't heist the ice," he said.

"I'm not accusing you of anything. I just want to get some information."

"My seminar didn't provide you with enough? Then try the stuff on the tables. It's all reasonably priced—some's even free. Better yet, Luna, why not subscribe to my online newsletter? You look like you can afford it, with those heels, the high-end shoulder bag...,"

"Please, Mr. Kuhl."

Lono sensed Luna's weariness and slowed his incessant sales pitch. A smaller portion of his generous smile returned, as Lono finished itemizing Luna's wardrobe. "...the white skirt and jacket—where you from, The Big Apple, Beantown..?"

"Oklahoma," Luna answered.

"No joke? I got a seminar planned for Tulsa. That's a classy city, with art museums, ballet—you're from there, I bet." The businessman extended his hand. "By the way, call me Lono."

"Just call me," the insurance investigator said, placing only a business card in Lono's hand.

Luna turned and headed for the exit when she felt someone behind her. It was Lono. "Hey, I'm sorry, Luna. Want to have a drink? I'll talk story to you that way."

"*Talk story?*"

"Sorry. It's just slang for chat." Lono lifted his wrist to get the time from his watch.

Luna noticed the timepiece. "A gold-cased Transocean Breitling ... nice," she said.

Lono took it off and tossed it like a toy to her. "*What the ...?!*" Luna gasped.

"We're not engaged or anything, "Lono laughed. "Just collateral on our conference, you might say. So, meet me at the bar in, oh, an hour. I got to break everything down and return the room in good condition."

True to his word, Lono showed up in the Marriott Suites Bar and Grill. He spotted Luna at a back-wall booth and walked over. Lono slid in across the table from her. Luna returned his watch.

"Thanks," Lono said, putting the Breitling back on. "You've got a sharp eye, noticing right off the bat what brand this was."

"And you've got good taste in fashionable and functional timepieces," Luna complimented Lono.

The waitress arrived and. Lono ordered Hawaiian mead. Luna hadn't tried mead before and ordered the same.

"It's a shame what happened to Pacific Splendor, huh?" Lono started to say.

Luna planted her elbow on the table and dropped her chin in her palm. "Tell me about it," she groaned. "The company that I represent is on the hook for $15 million, if it doesn't turn up."

"Got any idea where it might be—any suspects, besides me?"

"A few others," Luna said quietly.

"Well, I got more than a few for you, Luna: A.L.O.H.A."

"Leaving so soon, Lono?"

He gave Luna a slight grin and replied, "Funny," before becoming serious. "This A.L.O.H.A.'s a group of crazies that live up in the hills, north of The Town. They want to split from the fabulous 50. Maybe they thought that sinking the ship would get them more publicity. It did all right: One of their guys getting blown to bits probably has every fed spying on them now!"

"You know the ocean, Lono. Tell me: Could someone have dived down to that wreck before the Navy?"

"*And live to tell about it?!* Not without some serious diving equipment. I'm talking about deep sea submersibles or diesel, nuke subs. Two thousand feet of water is just too much pressure for a normal dive. Besides, I saw the raising on TV. The safe wasn't open when it first came up."

"Good point," Luna groaned.

"I think A.L.O.H.A.'s nuts enough to blow up a ship, but not nuts enough to try salvaging Pacific Splendor ahead of the feds, Luna."

"You're Hawaiian, not a local, right, Lono?"

"Yeah," he said. "Don't let my last name fool you. It's a holdover from my surfing days. It rhymes with "cool" and is a shout-out to the German culture out here. One of them was my first surfing sponsor."

"Why do you think A.L.O.H.A.'s "nuts," Lono? They did approve of the return of Pacific Splendor to Hawaii for safe keeping and having you, a Hawaiian, store it."

"My rump's not stamped with their seal of approval! Don't get me wrong: I appreciate what they did, in getting us more rights to claim minerals. But, Luna, they don't know when enough is enough. If we split from the Mainland, what do we get? I'll tell you: A new pimp-daddy country moving in and telling us what to do. *No thanks!* I'll stick with the devil I know."

The orders of Hawaiian mead and a bowl of Macadamia nuts arrived. Luna picked up the tab; and then, her glass. She offered a toast: "To the health of Pacific Splendor."

"You're always on the clock, aren't you?" Lono

laughed. Then, he clinked his glass with Luna's. After a couple of hearty swallows of the golden brown brew, Lono admitted, "Well, I'm always working, too. This business ain't easy. Gems, especially diamonds, are hard to explain to the average guy and gal. They're also hard to price and getting harder to find. But, that guy Sabal found over 110 carats over on The Big Island...*out of the blue, it seems!*"

Luna took a sip of mead and said, "I did a little digging into diamonds on my flight out here. What I read, and what you said tonight, confirms that red diamonds are real. Even more is that diamonds of all types can crop up just about anywhere in the world. Like on the Mainland: Arkansas has quite a few diamonds. And I was shocked when you said that Canada has a lot, too."

"The key phrase is that diamonds can be found "just about" anywhere in the world," Lono kindly reminded Luna. "Sure, diamonds are in lots of places. But not all are gem quality. Take the volcanic soil around Hawaii: It's full of tiny nanodiamonds. But, they're not jewelry-grade. For the most valuable stones, you need lots of old volcanic activity that brought them close to the surface centuries ago. And while the magma that carries them up is a special kind that erupts in an even rarer vent, the secret is pressure. Diamonds are really just pressurized carbon, Luna, from far beneath the Earth. The best ones—the one like Sabal found—usually come from 90 miles or deeper. Besides Hawaii not having diamond-making magma, there aren't vents that deep here."

"So you're saying that Rupee Sabal's find is scientifically impossible?" Luna asked.

"There are always exceptions in science. And with barely 30 red diamonds found, what do we really know about them? Like seahorses: The males have babies! And a platypus: It lays eggs like a bird," Lono said. "As a matter of fact, a few were found not too far from here: In Australia."

Luna plucked a nut from the bowl and asked, "Just "a few" platypuses in Australia, Lono?"

"No, I mean red diamonds: A few of *them* were found in Australia."

"So, it's possible that bigger diamonds, even red ones, are on the islands, but..."

"It's not real likely," Lono responded.

"Just like it's possible that you could win the lottery, but don't bet on it?" Luna offered.

Lono chuckled heartily, "That was a good line, Luna."

The insurance investigator lifted her glass and smiled.

"Well, I feel like I won the lottery with Gems of the Rim and Fort Rocks. And it would have been nice to hit it again, handling Pacific Splendor."

"About Fort Rocks: What's in it, Lono?"

"My clients' gems and jewelry," he answered. "Yeah, it's a big building. But, I bought it with plans for making it into a museum—maybe even an arena, too, after tonight. That crowd you saw would've been 3 or 4 times as big, if Pacific Splendor turned up for show and then storage."

"But your *show* saved the day," Luna replied.

Lono munched a handful of nuts and nodded. "I admit that I'm a rookie in the business—a cut-up who cuts in on other gemologists' and appraisers' territory. But, that's the upside of being an American: Free enterprise, right? I still give my customers honest advice, pay my people wages that are consistent with those in the industry..,"

"And, you're willing to "talk story" to pushy insurance people like me," Luna added.

"I wouldn't say "pushy", Luna," Lono said between sips. "You're just doing your job, and I'm doing mine. So, where's the harm?"

Luna lifted her glass. "Apparently, not where I thought it was," she sighed.

CHAPTER 16

A Serious Blow

Nani spent the next day trying to get information out of the remaining passengers and crew of *The Shilpa*. But it was difficult. Most only saw the diamond on TV. Others knew nothing about Pacific Splendor (besides that their vacation variety of it was ruined). Nani suspected that the cruise line probably promised bigger payouts on property claims; so, passengers shut-up about the condition of the ship. Late in the day, however, Nani finally got a break. Three crewmembers came to the Indian consulate with interesting information.

"So, Rupert Sabal lost $50,000 at the blackjack table?" Nani sought to confirm the allegation of the onboard casino worker.

Through Narmata's translation, he answered, "Yes. He is wealthy and well-known; so, maybe he could afford to lose that much. But, I have observed many card players during my time as a dealer. And

Rupert didn't seem like a professional. He seemed to want to be seen playing, not playing to win the game. My advice to Rupert: Stick to cricket."

"Do you have any other information?"

"Rupert was in the presence of someone quite often, at least during his visits to the casino."

"Who was it?"

"I do not know his name, only that he was a rather tall man with muscles," the casino worker answered. "But when I think about it, he could have simply been an admirer, as there were many who asked Rupert for his autograph." The casino worker didn't have any other information that Nani felt was related to Pacific Splendor. She thanked him and he left.

The next to enter was a short, stocky woman who had a tough look and spoke English. She identified herself as Alsia Aapt, *The Shilpa's* head of security. Nani directly asked if anyone else opened the safe or had access to the combination.

"No," Alsia said. "I changed the computerized combination each night so that even if someone stole it one night, the following night it would be invalid."

Nani asked Alsia if anyone else had access to the safe.

"Only I," Alsia answered proudly.

Nani continued. "As the head of security, did you notice anything suspicious onboard?"

Alsia thought for a minute. "No," she replied. "The passengers were well-behaved."

"What about the people around Rupert? Ever notice a tall man with muscles?"

"Do you mean a bodyguard?"

"Maybe," Nani replied.

Alsia dismissed the idea. "Rupert played cricket; he could take care of himself."

"But perhaps he needed someone to control his fans, Ms. Aapt."

"Fans?"

"Admirers of his cricket play," Nani clarified.

"Oh, I understand. I saw no one with Rupert, when he placed the diamond in the safe. And, as *Shilpa* sank, it was I who had to stop him from trying to return below to reclaim the diamond."

"Thank you, Ms. Aapt," Nani said.

Alsia took out a pen and wrote something on a piece of paper. She handed it to Nani and said, "This is my number to call, should you have more to ask of me."

The final crewman to enter wasn't as well-dressed and mannered as the previous two. He was barely 20 years old and wore a grungy T-shirt and jeans. Narmata looked at him dismissively. Nani knew that he probably didn't have a way home (wherever that was). The crewman was assigned to clean the engines. *This could be a big find!* Nani thought. She flashed the crewman a warm smile and patted his hand sympathetically when he sat at the table. "Thank you for taking the time to talk with me," Nani said. "You've been through a lot, haven't you?"

The worker nodded. "Do you offer a reward for information about the sinking?" he asked through Narmata.

"I'm interested in the missing diamond," Nani specified. "If what you know helps us find it, I've been authorized to say that my company will pay $10,000."

The worker's eyes widened and he wet his lips. *That was a fortune!* His lips then opened. "Okay. If I tell you this, I-I must have protection," he warned.

"I haven't heard anything yet that might justify protection or $10,000," Nani remarked.

The worker couldn't let this opportunity pass. "Okay. I saw Rupert Sabal talking with the head engineer."

Nani leaned forward and asked, "How much and what about?"

"I do not know what about. But I would say that they became friends. They would practice cricket moves on the deck. To do this, the engineer would often not be on duty. He would tell us what to do, but then something new would appear. So we could not continue with our work, until he arrived again to show us."

"Was the engineer on duty the night *The Shilpa* sunk?" Nani asked carefully.

The worker hesitated. Nani repeated the question. The sweat began to bead on the worker's brow.

He thought of how the engineer yelled at him and how $10,000 could erase those memories and make better ones for his family back home. "I did not see him on my shift," he blurted out.

"And your shift was during the exact time the ship sank?"

"Yes, ma'am. I believe something happened in the engine room. I do not know what. But I do know that I barely made it from there alive!"

Nani thanked the worker. He hesitated, and then left the room. Narmata turned to Nani. "It is perhaps not my place to say this, but some of these workers..."

"I know, I know: They might say anything for the reward money," Nani interrupted.

"Money is something that can be understood without an interpreter, yes?"

"There's always one question to translate, Narmata: What are you paying me to do?"

"The card dealer did not help Rupert win, and the man he saw with him did not cause harm. The security guard did not open the safe to anyone and said that she had to keep Rupert from returning for the diamond. And the boy in the engine room only said Rupert engaged his supervisor in cricket. He "did not see him" on duty, but that does not mean his supervisor was not helping other workers elsewhere. So, I fail to see any wrongdoing aboard *Shilpa*," Narmata said.

Nani smiled. "For what it's worth, Narmata, I agree," she replied. "But, there are people who might not."

Narmata asked, "Do you mean Luna?"

"Yes," Nani said. "She deals with criminals more than we do, and would say that there are more people than one pirate involved. I can't say that she would blame *The Shilpa* crew, but who knows? I do agree with her that criminals and their motives are not easy to quickly pin down."

"Then perhaps I will stick to translating easy to understand dialects," Narmata concluded.

Nani asked if the three crewmembers had to be kept at the Indian consulate. Narmata said that the casino dealer was from Calcutta; so, she was confident that his stay would be approved. The head of security was from near Panna, India; so she was probably welcome, too. But, the engine room worker was a refugee from Bangladesh (and not exactly versed in Emily Post). So, until she could "get authority to approve his stay," he couldn't remain in the facility. "But, you may take the boy to the Bangladesh consulate, Nani," Narmata suggested.

Nani piled the engine room worker into her car. But before starting out, she took out her smartphone and made a phone call. Once en route, the jewelry appraiser made another call. "Luna," Nani said, "We found three key witnesses from *The Shilpa*."

"*Great!* Where are you?" Luna wanted to know.

"I'm on my way home with one of them: An engine room worker."

"Here?!"

"Why not? You wanted to ease off a bit, right Luna? And we've got this guy's testimony that, among other things, he's at least 18." Static began to sizzle through the reception. "I'm just kidding, Luna. I'm bringing him home because…"

The static increased. "Nani, you're breaking up. Listen, don't…" Suddenly, the connection dropped off. Apparently, Nani was out of cellular range. Luna tried to re-dial. Nani didn't answer.

Meanwhile, rush hour traffic out of downtown Honolulu began to let-up a bit, enough for Nani to speed up and cross into the middle lane. She didn't pay much attention to a motorcyclist who also increased speed. The rider was in the fast lane, but slowed to Nani's speed. Nani glanced over and saw the motorcyclist (dressed in black and a shielded helmet) looking at her. She didn't think much of it. The motorcycle slowed to a spot just behind Nani's driver side rear. A sudden thought popped into Nani's mind: The morning she got the newspaper, a motorcycle buzzed by. Nani quickly dismissed the thought. Her attention returned to the road, where the motorcyclist had since drawn a cellphone and, with the press of one of its buttons, first blood.

BOOM! Nani's front tire exploded. She slammed on the brakes, but swerved right. The car was hit twice, before crashing into the northbound retaining wall. From an over the shoulder glance, the motorcyclist saw traffic grind to a halt and smoke rise in the distance. Confident that the other side had been dealt a serious blow, the motorcyclist revved up and raced away.

CHAPTER 17

Soldier on

Luna arrived at Oahu Mercy Hospital. The emergency room was full of frantic families, some from the highway pile-up that Nani's blowout caused. After a few minutes, Luna found out that Nani was in surgery (which meant a long wait for any word). She calmed down and took a seat in the hallway. But the longer Luna waited, the more she stewed. So, after a while, she left for the cafeteria.

The walk to the elevator and the ride down got rid of the cramps from sitting. When Luna stepped out, she noticed that the cafeteria was closed. So, she went to the vending machine and punched out some guava juice. The smooth taste suddenly reminded her of the first time it was served: By Nani. After that thought, the only liquid to flow were tears. Luna threw the can into the trash and cursed herself: *"Damn you, for getting Nani in so deep! I should have let her simply be "a good hostess!"*

Some people passed by, snapping Luna back to the present. She hurried to the restroom; then, wiped her face; and leaned toward the mirror for a long look at herself. Once Luna finally saw a solid insurance investigator surface, she left.

When Luna returned upstairs, the face of another person waiting in the emergency room corridor looked familiar. Luna approached the Filipino man carefully. He looked up. "Hey," he said. It was the man from Nani's fancy-framed photograph. Only now, his smooth face was etched with crow's feet. And his once glossy, black hair was rumpled, along with his polo shirt and khakis.

"Hi," Luna replied. "Are you here for Nani Nyoko, too?"

"Yeah, I'm a business associate."

"You're from Safe Pacific, right?"

"*Who are you?!*" the man asked grouchily.

"Nightcrow, Luna Nightcrow. I'm an insurance investigator, also contracted by Safe Pacific. Nani was—is, I mean—helping me to find the diamond."

The Filipino man finally introduced himself as, "Miguel Diamante: I'm the gemologist who Safe Pacific contracted to handle Pacific Splendor."

Luna bit her lip and shook her head. "I-I'm sorry for being so business-minded, at a time like this."

"Forget it," Miguel replied. He looked down at the floor and then at his hands. "If I had that diamond, I'd trade it to anyone right now for Nani's recovery."

"That makes two of us," Luna agreed. She took a seat beside Miguel, and noticed he reeked of stale beer and cigarette smoke. After a moment Luna asked, "You two are friends?"

"We're friendly. The jewelry biz is big-time and cut-throat, so I don't have many "friends.""

"Worked a lot of cases with her?"

"Just this one," Miguel said. "But, we were together a lot: Going through the books, making calls, and taking calls. A lot of work goes into cutting a stone." Then, Miguel's blood-shot eyes looked at Luna suspiciously. "Did Nani say we were an item or something?"

Luna laughed a little. "No, Miguel. She said that you were just co-workers."

"Good. Us working with that diamond so much might have given her the crazy idea that I was going to buy her one. Women see so much stuff that isn't there!"

"*Yeah, sure!*" Luna snorted. Then, she reminisced. "I'm staying with Nani. I-I kind of envy her nice home, the view, how she cooks so well..."

"Where are you from?" Miguel asked rather sharply.

"Oklahoma," Luna replied.

"Living here must seem like Shangri-La to you: Just fun and sun 24/7, huh?"

"Until lately," Luna remarked, suppressing a sniffle.

"Well, it's a gilded cage, Lightcrow—I mean, Nuna. It costs a lot of money, when nearly everything is shipped in from someplace else. A lot of the Hawaiians are mad about the food prices, the high utilities, the clogged-up roads..."

Luna dared to ask, "Which Hawaiians?"

"Come on, Luna, don't give me that! You know who I'm talking about."

"Yeah," she replied. The insurance investigator opened her handbag and pulled out a business card. "Look, Miguel, this isn't the best time to talk about the case, I know. So, just call me when things...when it's convenient, okay?"

After a minute, Miguel looked up from the floor and at Luna. He finally took the card. "You know, I auditioned for that musical *Oklahoma!* once," Miguel said. Then he grinned, and Luna noticed a faraway look in the gemologist's eye. "But, I couldn't cut it on Broadway..,"

"So, you started cutting diamonds instead, huh?"

Miguel nodded. "The Diamond District wasn't too far off. Wandered over—first thought about robbing a store, I was so broke and hungry! But, the owner gave me a job cleaning up. After a while, I read up on gem cutting. Looked like something anybody could do. The owner got his training in India; so I went there and got mine at I.C.E."

"You mean, Independent Cutting & Confirmation Enterprises?" Luna sought to verify.

"Cool name, huh?" Miguel chuckled. "Saw Rupee Sabal a few times over there. He dug my work on his pals' bling. But, I set up shop and got a degree in gemology here—more Filipinos here, better beer, too. When Rupee blew through and found the stone, he looked me up to cut it."

"And what a cutting job you did on it," Luna praised Miguel.

Miguel grinned and then looked into Luna's eyes. "Not beautiful as nearly the good-looking job they did on you. You're rocking my world right now, Nuna Lightcrow!"

And you really thought this guy was such a hunk?! Damn, Luna! When this thing is over, you need to take a course on properly appraising male potential! she told herself.

"Appraising" returned thoughts about Nani. Suddenly, the doors shielding surgery opened. A tired, thin-faced man of 45, who looked 55, appeared. But, he put on a practiced professional air when he approached Luna and Miguel. "Are you friends or family of Nani Nyoko?" he asked, in what Luna thought sounded like an Australian accent. Both nodded anxiously without identifying themselves. "I'm Dr. Owen Madison. I won't beat about the bush: Ms. Nyoko is in serious but stable condition. The air bag and her seat belt kept it from being much worse. However, she suffered broken bones, lacerations, and has head trauma from collisions from oncoming traffic."

Miguel's eyes widened. "Who did this, doc? A drunk, some teen-aged kid, an old fart…?"

Luna softly grasped Miguel's arm, and he got the signal to calm down.

"I don't know all of the circumstances, sir. But I can say that Ms. Nyoko suffered a Grade III concussion, meaning she lost consciousness from the accident. The extent of damage to the brain won't be known for some time, but expect immediate side effects such as confusion, moodiness, and quite possibly post-traumatic amnesia," the doctor explained.

"Was she driving by herself, doctor?" Miguel asked.

"A male passenger in Ms. Nyoko's car didn't survive," Dr. Madison answered.

Miguel persisted. "Was he a relative or friend?"

"Neither," Luna responded. "Thanks, doctor, for the news."

Doctor Madison nodded and left. Miguel sighed and dropped into his chair. But Luna's mind raced and her nerves tightened. She had to soldier on. And, as usual, it looked like it would have to be as an army of one woman.

CHAPTER 18

Island-hopping

Luna returned to Nani's house early the next morning. She collected the mail from the day before and turned off the lights. Luna then checked her e-mail and found the transcript of *The Shilpa* crewmembers' testimony. She read it and then called Narmata Buddhiman.

"Luna, I am so sorry to learn of Nani Nyoko's accident," the interpreter said. "She is alive?"

"Yes, and thanks for your concern," Luna replied. "I received your transcripts, Narmata. They were very informative."

"I am glad, Luna," Narmata replied. "You may also be happy to know that the Consul General approved the security officer and casino worker's stays, if they want to remain. We would like to have hosted the engine room worker as well, but there are political considerations that made it impossible. My translation of his testimony was good will towards the people of Bangladesh and to help your effort to recover Rupert Sabal's diamond. But, Bangladeshis have their own consulate in Honolulu. To keep the boy here might be perceived as though we were keeping him—questioning him—against his will."

"And the fact that his testimony seems to place the blame for *The Shilpa* sinking on the engineer's negligence wouldn't make him a popular guest at the Indian consulate," Luna added.

"I did advise Nani to take him to the Bangladesh consulate. Were they driving there?"

"I don't know," Luna sighed.

"I hope Nani gets better, Luna. And I hope you appreciate and understand our actions."

"I do," Luna said. "You did a good job, Narmata, and I'll be in touch. Namaste."

After taking a shower, Luna dressed and rang the Honolulu Police Department for the police report on Nani's car accident. Detective Sergeant Ernesta Valerosa handled the case and reported that an investigation was underway. But, she gave no further details (besides what was reported on the news). After breakfast, Safe Pacific Property and Maritime Insurance called Luna with the analysis of Rupee's cricket bag sample. Other than a little dirt, the lab found a trace of lead in the polyester fabric; but, nothing consistent with diamonds. Luna thought, *Lead and dirt*: Probably just paint from the gear and soil from the field. Luna also asked for a breakdown of Rupee's cargo insurance policy. Finally, she took the opportunity to put in a good word for Nani. "She's been invaluable," Luna told the Safe Pacific representative.

Just before noon, the insurance investigator picked up her smartphone again. She found the number she was looking for from the online Yellow Pages. But before her fingers could dial, her senses were awash in last night's events—in the emergency room, specifically. Luna planned to call Miguel Diamante. But she remembered the smell of booze and smoke and his moodiness. He's probably hung over, Luna thought. So, she dialed another number instead.

"Gems of the Rim Investment, how may I direct your call?" the receptionist answered.

"Mister Kuhl, please. This's Luna Nightcrow, independent insurance investigator working for Safe Pacific Property and Maritime Insurance, Honolulu."

"One moment please, Ms. Nightcrow."

Luna liked the jazzy on-hold music. But, it was shortly replaced by the more likable tone of Lono Kuhl. "Aloha, Luna," he answered.

"Good morning, Lono."

"I heard about Nani Nyoko. Is she any better?"

"She's in serious but stable condition. It could have been a lot worse."

"Yeah," Lono said. "Well, whatever you need for your investigation, you let me know."

"That's why I called, Lono," Luna said. "I'd like to

visit the location where Pacific Splendor was found—specifically, to take soil samples."

"Sure thing," Lono said. "I have a plane on retainer. Want me to pick you up?"

"In the plane?!"

Lono laughed, "No, in my car. The plane is for where we'll be going."

"No, thanks," Luna declined. "I'll be by in an hour. Is that okay?"

"Perfect. Meet me in Lot D2 at Honolulu International. Oh, by the way, do you have hiking shoes?" Lono asked.

Luna moaned, "In that case, make it two hours; I need to go shopping."

Ala Moana Center was only 7 miles from the airport. So, Luna stopped at the large, open-air mall to shop. She finally arrived at Honolulu International around 1:30 pm. Luna parked and looked for Lono. Soon, the tall Hawaiian came into view. He was dressed in shorts, a T-shirt, and hiking shoes and carried a small, metal suitcase. Lono grinned at Luna's more rugged choice of jeans, camp shirt, and boots. She lugged her new backpack and big canteen over to his car.

"I thought you were just buying shoes!" Lono said.

Luna shrugged. "Reliving my Girl Scout days, I guess," she laughed.

"This will probably a few hours trip, with most of it spent flying and driving to the site."

"I remember another such trip...aboard *The Minnow*: "A three hour tour, a three hour tour.""

Lono recognized the line from the old *Gilligan's Island* song and laughed, "Don't jinx us!"

The two found the hangar for a sleek, twin engine Piper Mojave aircraft. Lono and the pilot spoke briefly. The pilot then continued with his pre-flight checks, while Luna and Lono stowed their gear and climbed aboard. The white-walled cabin was roomy, with navy blue carpet, six comfortable leather seats, and mahogany pullout tables. Luna and Lono sat in facing chairs and strapped in. About ten minutes later, the pilot climbed aboard. The Piper's engines coughed and the propellers whirled. Slowly, the plane taxied onto the runway. And moments later, it lifted into clear, blue sky and headed for Hawaii, The Big Island.

Lono unfolded a map and draped it over the pullout table. Luna leaned forward for a closer look. Lono pointed out a spot and said, "Where we'll be looking is in a river valley."

"Not a volcano?" Luna asked. "I thought diamonds mostly come from volcanic areas that force them up from deep within the Earth."

"You really got to subscribe to my newsletter online, Luna," Lono teased. "Yeah, the bigger ones usually do come from old volcanic areas. But, they can come from other places, too. Pacific Splendor is an alluvial. It's a fancy term for a gem that's been carried from the original place it was released, usually by water here in Hawaii. Anyway, they are harder than most rocks and collect on the bottom of riverbeds along with sand and mud.

"A few Hawaiians and locals used to pan for alluvials back in the day, just like prospectors on the Mainland used to pan for gold. Now, there aren't really enough valuable ones out here to bother with. To help boost tourism, the state created this site for tourists to dig for olivine."

Luna was surprised at how quick the flight between Oahu and Hawaii was. In less than an hour, the plane landed at Hilo International. Luna and Lono got out and the pilot helped them unpack their gear. They took a jeep to the airport rental car company (where Lono's surfing celebrity got them a top-of-the-line Range Rover).

Lono followed Highway 19 from Hilo into increasingly wooded hills and valleys. After about a half an hour, he finally pulled off at the pay-to-mine park. Luna and Lono unpacked their gear and proceeded to the park office. Luna paid the fee, and finally they were ready to begin. Lono led Luna along a narrow, dirt trail that curled through a garden-like landscape of green ferns and tropical trees whose canopies vanished in a gathering, overhead mist. The trip ended at a rocky ravine that was wet by the silvery ribbon of a small waterfall that trickled from the canyon walls.

"Eureka!" Lono announced. He knelt and unpacked his equipment.

Luna stopped and simply marveled at what seemed like land untouched by time. She took a seat on a big, mossy rock and became lost in thought. She watched Lono's strong arms and nimble fingers dig through the brown mud and gravel. Luna thought of them preparing a hook to catch a fish or searching for stones to fashion a spear from; and then, of how he would wrestle to bring in the wild, thrashing animal. But, she snapped out of her daydream when she saw Lono look up.

"You find playing in dirt that interesting?" he asked.

Luna smiled. "Not as much the dirt as you," she explained. "I guess that seeing you digging around in shorts isn't what I expected, from a big-time jewelry CEO."

"Well, the way you wore that suit the other night and kept the conversation all about business was classy. In a place full of bikinis and beach bunnies, you turned my head, instead."

"Insurance usually just turns most people's stomachs," Luna said softly, distantly.

Lono stopped working and approached her. He pulled out a red hibiscus he'd plucked along the trail. Lono caressed Luna's hair and tucked the flower behind her ear. "Feel better?" he asked.

Luna smiled and nodded. "I've seen that done

so many times on TV and thought it was so corny. But now...thanks, Lono," she said. "I just wish I had a flower for you, too."

"*What?!* And ruin my reputation as a hard-ass?" Lono replied.

"You're not a "hard-ass"; but a smart-ass, yes!" Luna kidded.

Lono returned to collecting riverbed samples. About 10 minutes later, he heard Luna call out, "Lunch is served." A table cloth was spread over one of the big, flat-topped rocks and arranged on top was a light lunch of fruit, spam, rice, and a thermos of Kona. Lono grinned and joined Luna on one of the facing boulders. He washed his hands with water from her canteen and began eating.

After a while, Luna's thoughts returned to the diamond. "Maybe that's why A.L.O.H.A. is so up in arms: If there's another big gem haul, tourists and the government will destroy all of this."

"Sounds like you share Joni Mitchell's fear: "Pave paradise and put up a parking lot.""

"If it was just one, maybe there wouldn't be need to worry."

"Relax, Luna. This's just another tourist trap: One for people who hate the beach."

"Why did you ever get into the jewelry industry?" Luna asked Lono.

"I wish I had some brilliant answer. But, it comes down to being past my surfing prime. I got a degree in geology that I decided to dust off, after 16 years, and put to some use," he answered.

"No gemological or appraisal training?"

"I got enough to compete. But don't let that stuff fool you, Luna. Gemologists and appraisers know the cuts, the prices—the end game. But geology gives me a backstage pass to what uncut stones and minerals look like in the ground, their structures, and so on." Then, Lono asked, "About gems and appraisers: Do you think that what happened to Nani was an accident?"

"Lono, I don't want to involve you in this any more than I have," Luna said firmly.

"*Hey!* I've surfed some pretty tough waters, from Mavericks to the Banzai Pipeline and even the beaches in Portugal. Even dealt with a few surf Nazis…"

Luna's brow wrinkled. "*Surf Nazis?*" she asked.

"Finding the best waves is harder than finding the best gems. So, some guys start gangs to "protect their surf," so to speak. Now, if I can handle that, I can handle this. I got your back, Luna."

Diamonds may be a girl's best friend. But until you have one, deal Lono in! Luna told herself. He's not just handsome, but he's tough and knows his stuff. After a long silence, she gave in. "Okay, Lono. But just know that what happened to Nani wasn't an accident. The kid in her car was a witness to shenanigans onboard *The Shilpa*. Now, I'm a target and so is anyone helping me."

"At six-foot-three, two hundred and thirty pounds of man, I can be a pretty beefy barrier."

"Don't forget to add your brains to the package."

"Okay, two hundred and thirty-and-a-half pounds," Lono wryly revised his figures.

Luna smiled. But suddenly, the sound of crackling brush startled her. The sound came from the opposite bank of the riverbed. And when Luna turned, she saw leaves and branches still moving. Luna slithered down from the boulder and landed in the mud. She slipped, but picked herself up and burst for the bank. Lono followed, calling, *"Luna, wait!"*

The other side of the ravine was tangled undergrowth, with no trail to follow. But Luna tore her way through, making one of her own. She heard more crunches and saw a branch move, as if to wave. Luna found a sharp stick, ran over, and stopped. Suddenly, there was movement from behind. Luna whirled to see…*Lono!* He stopped and grinned. Luna turned to see what caused it. It was the lunchtime intruder, dead ahead! It turned and scampered off, but it was on all fours.

"A deer!" Lono laughed: "All of that for a deer? Or maybe, Luna, you were just seeing if I can keep up with you, follow you anywhere."

"Or maybe, I find that a little exercise after lunch helps the digestion, Lono."

"But not your nerves: *Relax a little!* You almost broke your darned neck, and for what?"

"I thought it might have been an A.L.O.H.A. spy!" Luna shot back. After a moment, she let a tired laugh tumble out. "Rather paranoid of me, wasn't it?" Luna tossed her stick aside, turned, and looked up at Lono. "I'm sorry. Thanks for being in my corner," she said to him softly, openly.

Lono brushed the mud off Luna's shoulders and jeans, while she plucked the leaves and twigs caught in his hair during the chase. After managing to make each other look human again, Lono said, "Come on. If we're lucky, Luna, we can beat the deer, before he finishes our lunch."

If I catch that lurker near my lunch again, we can have him for dinner! Luna grumbled.

CHAPTER 19

Smooth Operators

Luna and Lono returned to the airport. In flight, Luna unpacked her first-aid kit and quietly tended to the nicks and scratches Lono sustained during her dash to catch what turned out to be A.L.O.H.A. apparitions. The Piper Mojave and its passengers safely landed back in Honolulu at 5:30 pm. At once, Luna called Oahu Mercy Hospital to check on Nani's condition. "She's conscious, but still too weak for visitors," Dr. Madison reported. So, Luna reluctantly stayed away.

Once in the parking lot, Luna got in her car; then, found the number Rupee last called from; and tried to give him a ring. But, the number was "disconnected or no longer in service." He's probably using pre-paid cellphones that can be thrown away, making tracking him difficult, Luna thought. But, as long as Rupee can file a claim, I can expect to hear from him.

Luna then rang Narmata Buddhiman at the Indian consulate, hoping to briefly review some of the surviving witnesses' testimony from Nani's inquest. Narmata informed her that Alsia Aapt left and didn't say where she was going. But, the casino worker was available. Luna spoke with him. Through Narmata's translation, she heard about Rupee's losses. But, Luna focused in on the tall man with muscles, asking if he was Indian. The casino worker's answer was, "Maybe, but I cannot be sure." Luna thanked him; then, Narmata; and hung up.

After returning to Nani's house, Luna washed her hiking clothes. She then changed into shorts and a tank top, before returning to her laptop and files for more research. Luna took the list of passenger names from the Coast Guard files. To her, they all *looked* like Indian names. Luna then decided to search for the names online. She hoped that maybe the passengers had social media sites or other Web links with photos. Luna found several, but nowhere near the 200 total. And none of the males looked similar to the robust bodyguard description. Of course, some of the pictures were dated. And muscles usually take time to develop.

At 7:30 p.m., Luna finally relaxed. She stretched, streamed some Michael Paulo smooth jazz from her laptop, and took a break for dinner. After eating,

Luna intended to take a cat-nap. But when she awoke on the couch, sunshine flowed through the living room window. And a look at her watch told her that it wasn't dawn's early light, but that of mid-morning. *Damned time difference!* the insurance investigator cursed to herself.

Luna headed for the shower. She undressed and turned on the water. But before even a toe could get wet, her smartphone rang. It was the Honolulu Police Department. Luna proceeded to quickly wash; then dress in her white skirt suit, floral blouse, and heels; and drive downtown.

At the station, the insurance investigator was met by Puerto Rican Detective Sergeant Ernesta Valerosa. Valerosa was shorter and younger than Luna. And her dress down day choice of jeans and a black golf shirt made her also seem more tomboyish. But, the two women shared similar bronzed features, dark hair, and (most importantly) determination.

Valerosa led Luna to a room whose decor seemed as innocent and ordinary as that of any office. But, the small size was a tip-off to Luna of its use: Questioning. Luna took a seat across from Valerosa at a table against the wall. The Detective Sergeant began by saying, "I want you to know that this is just standard procedure, Ms. Nightcrow. You're not a suspect."

"But, I know one of the victims: To the extent that I drove her car and then suddenly rented one of my own. Very suspicious—like I knew or planned the danger. Then, I still owe dough for damages done on an Iowa case — debt: Always a motive for wrongdoing." But then, the insurance investigator stiffened. "Of course, if the diamond is found, then I get paid much more than just expenses for not finding it. And without expert help—Nani's, precisely—to find it ..."

"All of that is true, Ms. Nightcrow," Valerosa cut in. "But, the main reason for asking you to stop by is to gather information. If you feel it's needed, you can have an attorney present."

Luna shook her head 'no.' So, the question-and-answer session began and went on for an hour and a half. Then, there was a knock on the door. Valerosa excused herself to answer it. Luna sat in the room, but not alone. As always, she had her thoughts to keep her company. For 15 minutes, Luna tried to fit the pieces of the case together. Then, the door opened again. "Ms. Nightcrow, please follow me," Detective Sergeant Valerosa asked.

The two women left the interrogation room. Valerosa guided Luna to the police garage. Luna stopped as they passed by the crumpled wreckage of Nani's Mitsubishi Mirage. After a moment of somber reflection, she continued on. The women finally arrived at a workbench, where Luna noticed a plastic pouch that contained a shredded rubber tube. Valerosa picked it up and handed it to the insurance investigator. "It turns out your fears of sabotage were right, Ms. Nightcrow," she confirmed. "The crime scene team found it."

Luna took the piece of shredded rubber and looked it over. "Some type of explosive, right?" she guessed.

Valerosa nodded. "It's a concentrated explosive filament. Someone removes the tire valve, inserts this thing, and then uses a small remote control with an antenna. The remote control acts on the same principle as a garage door opener: Point the device and it sends an open or close signal—only in this case, it's to the explosive for detonation."

"I know that a cellphone can be used to trigger bombs, system shutdowns, and overloads too," Luna said. "Cellphones are—hey, that reminds me, Detective Sergeant: Did you recover Nani's personal effects?"

"Yes," Valerosa answered, "and a smartphone was found among them. Now that this is a criminal investigation—a homicide investigation, at that—it's being held as possible evidence."

"Right," Luna replied. "My number will come up on the phone several times. But, can you let me know of any other calls that may have come in shortly before the time of the wreck?"

"I'll look into it, Ms. Nightcrow," Valerosa answered. The Detective Sergeant then returned her attention to the explosive. "I saw something like that, when I was in the Army. But now, with the increase in military surplus and even online weapons sales, it's a favorite toy of cowboy security companies and even above the board intelligence wet ops."

"Meaning that anyone could have bought one or even accessed websites on how to make one," Luna added. "Would it be easy for someone in a car to have detonated the tire?"

"Easier done from a motorcycle or moped," Valerosa responded. "No window to roll down, no arm sticking out to cause suspicion or panic. Anyway, Ms. Nightcrow, we'll check local surplus, pawnshop, and gun store purchases or inquiries into the device. I have a few military contacts I'll check with, too."

"Well, that narrows the suspects down quite a bit from mere street thugs to some pretty smooth operators," Luna replied, returning the bagged filament to Valerosa. "Besides me, who else do you have lined up for questioning?"

"Colleagues mostly," the Detective Sergeant replied. "Ms. Nyoko's parents are deceased. No brothers or sisters. Most of the other people are just those related to the case of the missing diamond, like the A.L.O.H.A. headquarters staff that you told us she talked to. As for the Bangladeshi ship worker, we're talking with the remaining crew and passengers of *The Shilpa*."

"If you need it, I have three crewmembers' testimonies, including the Bangladeshi's."

"That might be helpful. If we need those or

have further information, we'll contact you. Thanks again for your cooperation, Ms. Nightcrow."

"Thanks for keeping me in the loop, Detective Sergeant." As Luna turned to leave, she thought: *And I'm glad it's in the information loop, not the hangman's!*

Clear cut conclusion

Luna left the police station and returned to Nani's house. After slipping into shorts and a T-shirt, the insurance investigator dived into more research. Before Luna knew it, day had faded into dusk. She closed her laptop and went outside for the mail. After getting it, Luna was startled by the sudden appearance of a small, white-haired elderly woman wearing a lavender muumuu.

Luna thought she looked lost and walked over. "Aloha, ma'am, can I help you?"

"You are not Nani Nyoko," the woman said.

"No, I'm a friend."

"A girlfriend?" the woman asked.

Luna chuckled, "Oh, no! I'm just watching her house while..."

"...she recovers from her physical injuries," the woman interrupted.

Luna's eyes narrowed and she backed up. *"Who are you?"*

"May I please come inside for a glass of water? I have travelled a ways, Ms. Nightcrow."

The Godmother! Luna remembered Nani's term for A.L.O.H.A.'s leader Ailani Haku. The insurance investigator felt underdressed, in the presence of someone of such esteem. But then, she reminded herself that it was an esteemed crackpot—maybe even the woman who injured Nani! So Luna forgot about decency, but did extend some courtesy. Once inside, Luna offered Ailani a seat. She went into the kitchen, sat the mail aside, and got her guest the glass of water that she asked for. Ailani took a sip. "Thank you, Ms. Nightcrow," she said. The A.L.O.H.A. leader then studied Luna. "You are a Native American."

Luna nodded and answered, "A Cherokee."

"We share a similar history and a similar plight," the elderly woman said. "If my remembrance of history serves me correctly, your people fought with the South in the Civil War."

"Not our finest hour," Luna sighed, taking a seat across from the A.L.O.H.A. leader.

"You do not agree with their decision to leave the so-called "Union?"

"I don't agree with the South's reason for leaving:

To continue to have slaves. And not all Cherokee agreed with the alliance, by the way."

"But didn't some of your people have slaves?" Ailani countered.

"What people are perfect, Ms. Haku?" Luna asked. "On my flight here, I read about some of your people's history. There were issues between Pacific Island nations: Conquests occurred, tribes were wiped out.., but most of it done *before* the arrival of whites."

The last mouthful of water stuck in the back of the A.L.O.H.A. leader's throat. Her jaw tightened, as she forced more than just the liquid down. "We do not have much in common at all!"

"Yes, we do," Luna calmly maintained. "Both our peoples eventually had land—their culture—taken from them by outsiders, and did things that they hoped might get it back. Some of it was good, some bad. So, I more than understand where your anger and frustration come from.

"But, there is an English poem that says, "No man is an island, entire of itself. Every man is a piece of the continent, a part of the main." The world's becoming a smaller place, Ailani. We're becoming more dependent upon each other—united—regardless of what our ancestors did or had done to them. That poem was written centuries ago, but it means a lot to me."

"And to Nani, it might mean what?" Ailani asked.

"I think you know where Nani stands."

"I do now. But do you, Ms. Nightcrow?" After draining her glass, Ailani gathered her shoes. She seemed tired, not the matriarch that first tried to manipulate Luna. "It grows dark. I must go," she said. "Thank you for the water and for the conversation. You have a keen mind."

Luna managed a grin. "A benefit of being single: Time to think as you want," she said.

Ailani nodded. But then she sighed, "As time goes by and loved ones die, all you will want to think of is someone to share your thoughts with. "Heavy is the head that wears the crown."

Luna let Ailani have the last word—a pretty accurate remark from King Henry, at that. She walked Alani out, and watched her walk down the street and out of sight. Luna locked the door and re-entered the living room. There, she noticed a manila envelope on the coffee table. *That wasn't there before!* Luna lifted it and noticed that it was addressed to her. Carefully, Luna opened the clasp and shook the contents onto the coffee table. The first thing she saw was a small card with an embossed pineapple on it. Luna picked it up and flipped it open. Inside was a message that read, "When entering one's home, it is a custom to give a gift." *Ailani left the envelope!* Luna then looked at the other contents: Pages of invoices. But, they were all in Hawaiian—*great!*

Luna changed into her red satin short robe and prepared for a night of translation hard labor. But as she waited for the Hawaiian language dictionary to download, Luna remembered something about Ailani. The A.L.O.H.A. leader said she knew where Nani stood, but asked if Luna did. That spurred memories of Miguel Diamante: Specifically, his remarks about Hawaii's high cost of living and his concerns about who hit Nani and who her passenger was, rather than her condition. Then, Lono's words about finding Hawaiian diamonds flashed back. *Not real likely.*

Luna went to the kitchen and pulled out Nani's mail. She knew better than to open it. But from the mailing addresses, she noticed that most of it was bills: Collection notices, mortgage calls, and one past due utility reminder. Luna put the mail away, prepared a cup of Kona, and returned to the living room. She yawned and stretched out on the couch, but not to sleep. It was just a relaxing position from which to continuing thinking. At about 2 a.m., the clouds cluttering the insurance investigator's thoughts cleared. And a clear cut conclusion finally appeared.

CHAPTER 21

Salting the Earth

The strength of Luna's deductions depended upon what Lono Kuhl's samples from the Pacific Splendor site revealed. She didn't want to take the chance that something might happen to Lono or the facilities of Gems of the Rim. So, in the middle of the night, Luna threw on her T-shirt, jeans, and tennis shoes. Unsure of whether Ailani's surprise visit was paid in peace or to case the place, Luna gathered the Coast Guard evidence, her laptop, and the mysterious manila envelope. Then she locked up, hopped in her car, and sped off.

Luna killed the lights, as she pulled onto the grounds of the Gems of the Rim Business Park. The Fort Rocks Repository covered most of the area: Made of white granite and reinforced steel, it was surrounded by a high, barbed wired fence and monitored by banks of cameras. The main office complex looked like any other, bathed in the tawny glow of nighttime security lights and watched by a few cameras. Luna pulled into the back of the large main parking lot. Then, she took the smartphone from her handbag and sat it on the seat beside her.

Somewhere in a hazy dream about impossible things (like shouting to kids that dinner was ready) a phone rang. Luna's eyes opened to daylight streaming through the windshield. *It was morning!* Luna jumped up, looked out, and saw that Gems of the Rim was open. No ambulances or police cars. It looked like nothing happened to Lono overnight. The ringing of a phone sounded again. Only this time, Luna wasn't dreaming. Her smartphone was really ringing!

What is it? Maybe Nani's condition's worsened. Maybe the casino witness is dead. Maybe...maybe, I should just answer the damn phone, Luna concluded. "Hello?"

"Aloha, Luna, I have good news!"

Luna's shoulders dropped and her nerves eased off. *"Oh, Lono, you're okay!"* she gushed.

"Well, yeah," Lono chuckled. "Have a bad dream about me or something?"

Luna rubbed her eyes. "I wouldn't say that," she said. After all, those kids she called to dinner in her dream were Lono's and hers!

"Listen, Luna, I've been working on those samples, and found something that may make you feel better. Can you meet me here at the office?"

"I'm already in the parking lot!" she laughed.

Ten minutes later, Luna was inside Lono's office. She took out her Sony Xperia and Doro 410 mobile devices and began adjusting them, while Lono busied himself with translating the information from Ailani. Lono finished reading and asked Luna, "Okay, which of us goes first?"

"Normally, I'd say ladies," Luna said. "But since I can't report what I can't read, go ahead."

"These," Lono said, waving the manila envelope contents, "are just shipping reports. There's a rush delivery of $50,000 in loose diamonds from Panna, India to be delivered tonight at the Port of Honolulu. India buys, cuts, and ships lots of diamonds worldwide. So, I'm not sure what this has to do with Pacific Splendor."

"Who ordered them?" Luna asked.

"Miguel Diamante," Lono answered. "He cuts lots of diamonds, even Pacific Splendor."

Luna nodded and asked, "What about the samples from Hawaii?"

"This is where things get interesting." Lono separated Safe Pacific's documentation of the glittery, red diamond from his grungier soil samples. Then, he announced: "The good news is that Pacific Splendor is a real diamond and still worth eating money. Say, $20,000."

Luna gawked. *"Eating money?!"*

Lono smiled. "For me, I mean," he said. "The

bad news is that Pacific Splendor isn't from the islands. It looks like it's been enhanced on a couple of levels. One, someone tried to add local grains to the diamond; but, they're in the wrong concentrations. And two, since it's not from here, I'll bet the diamond really isn't red either, but colored red. That will drop the price, too."

"And you can tell all of that without the actual diamond to analyze?"

"I.C.E. and your insurance pros handled it. I'm just comparing their data to mine."

"Then where's Pacific Splendor really from, Lono?"

"When a diamond is cut, it loses a lot of natural flaws that would tell where it came from. But since they form at different geological stages, there are isotopes that are specific to the region they're from that get stuck in the diamond. I took out some sample stones from several of the big diamond producing areas around the world and looked for isotopes similar to those listed for Pacific Splendor. Most of the ones I found are close to here."

"How close?"

"Australia. But that's a hell of a travel here, even for an alluvial diamond."

"It was deposited, Lono, but not naturally. It sounds like salting: A scam I read about."

Lono nodded and said, "Where someone takes minerals from one place and plants them somewhere else, to trick miners into finding them and buying into what's really an empty mine."

"Or, it's done to increase the value of the diamonds used by the scammers," Luna added. "You did say, Lono, that olivine is the most valuable mineral at the pay-to-mine site. So, Pacific Splendor's scarceness made it all the more precious; and the area, that much more popular and profitable. And it probably explains why a shipment of $50,000 in additional diamonds is on its way here."

"What's the world come to, Luna, when a real diamond isn't good enough?"

"I'd better have a talk with a few people...*a serious talk*. And I'll need you in my corner again, Lono, in case things get rough."

Lono walked over to his desk and opened a drawer. He pulled out a .357 revolver and a belt holster. "Think this'll give the bad guys enough of a punch?"

The insurance investigator shook her head in disbelief. She showed Lono the mobile devices she worked on instead. "My cellphone is a rod and reel; and my smartphone, the bait."

"I don't get it," Lono said.

"Good."

"So now we're on a need-to-know only basis, huh?"

"Nothing personal, Lono."

He nodded and asked Luna, "So, which one of those is mine?"

"Neither. I'm the one fishing for information,

remember?" she said. "But, let me see *your* smartphone." Lono took out his smartphone and unlocked it. "You know about location services software for finding lost smartphones, right?" Luna asked him. Lono nodded. After working on his phone, Luna handed it back. "Thanks," she said, gathering the shipping report. "I'll be in touch."

"*Hey!*" Lono stopped Luna. "Want to grab a bite?"

"Maybe tomorrow," Luna said. "You've given me a lot to think about, Lono."

"So, you just need time to chew over it, instead of lunch?" he asked. Luna laughed. "Some other time, then," Lono finally complied. "But don't forget to breathe, Luna: You're human."

Luna lifted a finger to her lips. "*Shhh!* Don't tell anyone," she said. "I've got to catch a killer, find a diamond, and save my insurer from probably having $15 million."

"In that case, carry on, Wonder Woman!" Lono laughed.

"I liked her, until I got into insurance. Now, it's Batgirl."

"It's because of that bastard Bruce Wayne: All his stuff that you could insure!"

Luna winked. "That and Wonder Woman's damned invisible jet: It's so hard to find!" the insurance investigator griped. "Add to that airplane coverage and premiums that are sky-high."

CHAPTER 22

Harder Than Diamonds

The next day, Luna took Lono up on the offer of lunch. After calling him to find out the choice of restaurant, the description made her decide to dress business casual. Luna put on a T-shirt, jeans, and her skirt suit dress jacket. Then, she headed for the offices of Gems of the Rim. Halfway there, Luna's smartphone rang. She answered, "Hello?"

"Aloha, Ms. Nightcrow," Detective Sergeant Valerosa replied. "You wanted to know about any calls made shortly before the time of Nani Nyoko's wreck."

"What did you find?"

"Three calls: A call from Nani on the grounds of the Indian consulate; then one made to you, 5 minutes before the wreck; and the last was an unanswered call that went to Nani's phone."

"The two other calls: Who were the numbers registered to?"

"Alsia Aapt," Valerosa replied. "Does that help your case any?"

"She's the head of security for *The Shilpa*," Luna replied. "Nani questioned the ship passengers and crew about the whereabouts of the Pacific Splendor diamond."

"We've been unable to locate Aapt for questioning."

"I still have her testimony, and the offer to use it is still good."

"I think I'll take you up on that, Ms. Nightcrow."

"I'll e-mail it to you. And thanks, Detective Sergeant, for the news," Luna said.

The line dropped off, but Luna's thoughts didn't. Alsia probably gave Nani her number. But if they were both still at the consulate, why would Nani need to call? Why not just update each other inside or outside? Maybe one of them left early? Then Luna thought, Alsia is a security officer; her job is to protect things. And the call to Nani: Cellphones can be used to...*bingo!*

Luna filed her latest deduction, as the turn-off for Gems of the Rim appeared. *Breathe, Luna, breathe!* Lono's relaxation tip began to echo in the insurance investigator's mind, as she finally pulled into the parking lot. Waiting happily was Lono. Luna parked and met him at his Lincoln Navigator. It was beginning to get hot, so Luna removed her jacket. Before she could unwind further, her smartphone rang again. "Hello?" the insurance investigator answered tiredly.

"Good day, Ms. Nightcrow." This time, it was Dr. Madison. "I have terrific news: Ms. Nyoko's condition has been upgraded to fair. The police asked her a few questions. But, Ms. Nyoko asked for you and gave me your number to call."

"Did Nani ask to see a Mr. Diamante?" Luna wanted to know.

"Mr. Diamante?"

"The man I was with the night you spoke to us about her condition."

"I'm sorry, Ms. Nightcrow," Dr. Madison apologized. "But no, she didn't ask; and, to my knowledge, that man hasn't visited."

"I'll be by to see Nani shortly, doctor," Luna said.

So instead of the seafood restaurant, Lono pulled into the front parking lot of Oahu Mercy Hospital. Luna got out. "I'll be back in 15 or 20 minutes," she told Lono.

Luna rode the elevator up to Nani's room. She knocked and obeyed the soft "come in" from its occupant. The door opened and Luna entered to the usual outpouring of get well cards and potted plants. As for Nani, her right arm was in a sling and her left leg elevated and in a cast. Nani's face was nicked with cuts and abrasions. But she lit up as soon as she saw Luna. The insurance investigator delicately hugged her colleague and took a seat at her bedside. Luna grinned. "I feel stupid for asking this, but how are you feeling?"

"Lousy," Nani answered. "I think I need a stomach transplant: The food here is terrible!"

"I'd offer to cook you something, Nani, but I can't cook."

Nani smiled. "Wow! It's nice to know there's something you can't do, Luna. The way you carry yourself seems so...perfect."

"It's a blessing and a curse," Luna softly replied. "But, on the bright side, there's something I couldn't do that I'm becoming good at."

"*Oh, yeah?* Like what?"

"I've become quite the homemaker. I get your mail and turn the lights on and off."

Nani smiled. "Thanks, Luna."

"Speaking of the mail..." Luna placed her hand on Nani's and looked her in the eye. "...why didn't you tell me?"

"*About the bills?*" Nani asked. Luna nodded. "Because they're no big deal: Everybody gets behind sometime. Or, is this one of those things you can't do?"

"I've been behind...on solving this case."

"But, you're starting to catch up?"

"Catch on is perhaps a better word, Nani."

"Good, Luna. I told the cops that A.L.O.H.A. was a good place to start looking for the guy who did this."

"I talked to Miguel Diamante while you were still in surgery, Nani."

Luna noticed a change in Nani's face; and then, in her tone. "What did he want?" Nani asked.

"Just to make sure you're safe," Luna answered.

There was a long silence. Then, Nani snorted, "Just to see if I'd talk now or ever, you mean." Nani looked out the window. The sky was blue, and so was Nani's mood becoming (though it was to be a darker shade). "That silly picture you saw—Luna, Miguel and I shared a lot in common. I-I thought that we might be marriage partners, instead of business partners, someday."

"Instead, you're partners in crime," the insurance investigator said.

"When did you know, Luna?"

"Not right away. I thought your constantly trying to steer me towards A.L.O.H.A. as the perps was just an overreaction. But then I realized that Coast Guard evidence of the sinking and your description of the organization simply didn't fit typical pirate mo. Also, Pacific Splendor was returning to Hawaii—*exactly what A.L.O.H.A. wanted!* Ailani and her cronies won a political victory through protests and rhetoric. So, terrorism or piracy seemed crazy and ultimately suicidal.

"Next, a tip-off to fraud is excessive insurance coverage. It sometimes leads to sliding in extra fees or coverage without the customer knowing. You said that Rupee not only has a cargo policy that covers war acts, but a separate terrorism insurance policy. I don't think he would have paid twice for basically the same insurance. Also, I talked with Safe Pacific. They said there were additional fees for legal defense slipped in. Maybe that's why you kept exaggerating A.L.O.H.A.'s status as terrorists: To scare Rupee into buying extra coverage and then slide in hidden fees."

Nani tried to build a defense. "Not enough to link me to some diamond scam," she argued.

But Luna wasn't through. "What really made me suspicious of you was the wreck: It wasn't an accident," she added. "You told me that you appraised cars too. You've probably seen a lot of ways to fake damage and wrecks. The method that you or your accomplice chose was to plant a tiny explosive in your tire. The reason: To scare or kill the key witness to sabotage or dereliction of duty onboard *The Shilpa*. If the cops hadn't found the explosive, it would've officially been just another traffic accident. Narmata also told me that you could have taken the engine room witness to the Bangladeshi consulate. Instead, you risked bringing him to your house!

"But the clincher was the soil samples in Hawaii: They don't match the geological structure of Pacific Splendor. An experienced gemologist who cut the raw diamond would have seen that and told the appraiser it was salted. But Miguel's talk about Hawaii's high cost of living and it not being a paradise and me seeing all of your bills suggests that, in order to make money, you both covered-up the fact that Pacific Splendor wasn't from Hawaii. Maybe you two even enhanced the diamond and then planted it in the pay-to-mine river valley for Rupee to find."

Nani's patient smile cracked, and a confession came out. "Know what's harder than diamonds, Luna? The truth," she sighed. "The scam wasn't my idea. But yes: Miguel and I took bribes to increase the quality of Pacific Splendor in our grading reports. We both knew that not a lot is known about red diamonds. So, we added red coloring to a diamond. But, we added local grains to make it look like Pacific Splendor was from Hawaii, if someone challenged the find."

"And what about the wreck, Nani?"

"For a thousand dollars more, I leaked our investigation plan: That's how they knew about the engine room witness. I just thought they'd pay him off, not knock him off. The bomb or whatever must have been planted earlier. Maybe it was really for me."

"Or me," Luna replied. "You couldn't get me off the case, so maybe this was supposed to."

"Miguel probably thought that if he could fool the industry pro's, he could fool you: Someone who's not nearly as experienced in jewelry. *But fooling me?* I'm up to my neck in this mess. They probably thought that you and me were too friendly: That I switched sides."

Luna pressed Nani for more information. "You called Alsia Aapt at the consulate, just before calling me on the day of the wreck. She's a security officer: She protects not just places and things but people, too. Did Alsia follow you? Did she set-off the bomb with a cellphone trigger?"

"You know, Luna, that Aussie doc told me to expect some "post-traumatic amnesia." So you'll understand if I *don't remember*."

"Your memory's been fine, until..,"

"Don't push it, Luna! Any good attorney could twist this to my advantage!"

After a long pause, Nani calmed down. "I'll just say this," she said. "Appraising jewelry is like working at a bank. You have thousands of dollars going through your hands all damned day. But, you go home to a mailbox full of bills you can't pay. Then, one day, you say 'to hell with it' and go all-in with some handsome devil, for a few dollars more." Tears began to flow down Nani's cheek.

Luna hung her head. "I-I'm sorry, Nani."

"For what: Doing your job?!" Nani replied. "You're only "sorry" if you don't finish it. You got the bad girls; now, get the bad boys, too. Don't let them hang all of this on just me, Luna."

Luna nodded sadly. She stood, gave Nani a final hug, and left the room. Luna walked down the hall and turned the corner to the water fountain. When she rose from taking a drink, the insurance investigator felt something hard in her back. *"Don't turn around!"* a voice growled. "Walk with me to the stairs. It will be good for your health."

A cold sweat broke out across Luna's forehead. She did as the man told her. The two walked down the corridor and past one or two patients that happily said, "Hi, doc," to the gunman.

Oh, shit! Doctor Madison must have lured me here! Luna thought.

The two arrived at the stairwell. Luna opened the door and they descended three floors to the exit. The door opened into the hospital's rear parking lot. The man led Luna to a non-descript sedan. He opened the back door and pushed her in. Luna felt the back seat sink, as she turned to see that the man now beside her wasn't Dr. Madison. It was instead the big Hawaiian-looking man who chased her at the Waikiki Hilton. He now wore a doctor's white coat with scrubs underneath. And in his hand was a gun. At the wheel was another familiar face: Miguel Diamante's.

CHAPTER 23

Too Many Questions

The car started and so did more talking, this time from Miguel. The gemologist tossed his cigarette butt out the window, slipped on his Ray-Ban shades, and began to drive. "Figured it wouldn't be long before you showed up to put the squeeze on Nani," he told Luna. "Well, did she crack?"

"No," Luna replied. "Nani said she told the cops that it was A.L.O.H.A. who sunk the ship and caused her wreck."

"What did she blab to you about?"

"Only about how crappy the hospital food was."

"Think she was right, Nightcrow?"

"That's *Lightcrow*, remember Miguel? Anyway, I didn't get a chance to taste it."

"You'll get a chance to taste plenty of it: Through

a tube in a room next to Nani, if you keep getting smart!" the gemologist roared.

"Okay, Miguel, I told her that I knew the diamond's not worth what she appraised it for."

"And…?"

"And, Nani said that I was full of it and couldn't prove any of it," Luna lied. *"Satisfied?"*

"Sometimes, that Nani can be stronger than sapphire!" Miguel chuckled. "So enlighten me, Nightcrow. Who else knows about Pacific Splendor—I mean, *really* knows?"

"Whoever has it and runs a simple geological cross-check on it will know it's salted and enhanced," Luna guessed. "It was a clever scam, I'll give you that."

"Not just clever, but brilliant—*goddamned brilliant!*" Miguel boasted. "Scammed not just that sucker insurance company—no, that was too easy—but, we got it past the jewelry industry. That's the hardest part: Selling the Eskimo some ice."

"But why did you do it, Miguel?" Luna asked.

"Cost me $20,000 to become a Graduate Gemologist—20 grand, to end up fixing up old ladies' heirlooms mostly. Nobody's buying top drawer jewelry anymore. And tomorrow, synthetic gems will outsell the real deal anyway. Just give me one big payday, so I can get away from it all!"

"With Nani?"

Miguel shrugged. "Or without her," he answered Luna.

"If you and Nani cooked up this deal, do you think that you could make room at the table for another guest?"

He grunted, "Hungry, huh?"

"I have bread, but I'd like a little jam on it for once," Luna answered.

Miguel chuckled, "Want to taste the bigtime, huh? Well, Nightcrow, it's not my call. You'll have to talk to The Big Kahuna. What a brain, that Kahuna!"

"The Big Kahuna? Do you mean the people from I.C.E.?"

Miguel's smile faded. He squirmed in the driver's seat. "You're starting to ask too many questions, babe!" He glanced back at the hefty man. "Turn down her volume, will you?"

A grin creased the corners of the hefty gunman's mouth. *"Gladly!"* he grumbled.

Luna turned directly into the unforgiving glare of dark eyes that glittered like obsidian. Then her world turned sideways, violently so, as the hefty gunman shoved her across the backseat and into the door. Luna slowly straightened, but suddenly felt a sharp pain in her side that put her down again. The shock from being shot stifled a scream. Luna weakened, her eyes fluttered.

"That is what a real gun does!" the insurance investigator heard the hefty man mock her.

Then, Luna fell across the seat and succumbed to darkening silence.

CHAPTER 24

The Diamond Head Deception

Miguel Diamante pulled the sedan off the road. Everyone waited for the dust to settle. After a couple of slaps and shakes, Luna came to. The first thing she saw was the barrel of the hefty man's gun, pointed inches from her face. Luna wasn't sure if it still held tranquilizer darts or now bullets. So when the back door swung open and Miguel ordered Luna to "get out" she didn't put up a fuss.

Luna straightened and eased her sore body out of the car. When her vision adjusted to the sun's glare, she saw an abandoned, split level house in the distance and a series of barren hilltops ringing the horizon. Miguel moved in front and the feel of a gun in her back started Luna forward.

The trio set out, crunching over landscape that was mostly gravel (with only patches of green sprouting here and there). Along the way, a couple of rusted-out junk cars broke the blandness. Finally, the trio arrived at the rickety fence that surrounded the house. Miguel Diamante pushed open the gate, and the hefty gunman pushed Luna through. One by one, they climbed a stairwell to the first level. There, they passed an empty pool; then, walked onto a faded patio; and finally stopped in front of a single lawn chair. A hot wind rustled a weather-beaten awning overhead, stirring up more dust. Everyone waited. Then, from within the shadows of the house, someone approached. Once in view, Luna instantly recognized the face.

"Aloha, Luna," Rupee Sabal said, taking a seat in the lawn chair. Instead of a tux, he now wore khakis, a red Aloha shirt, and a smug smile.

"Congratulations on your promotion to "The Big Kahuna," Rupee," Luna snorted.

Rupee chuckled, "It is just a local word for "magician," I think. Anyway, how do you like my new "digs," as they also say?"

"No one will mistake this for the Waikiki Hilton, will they?"

"Glamor is what diamonds can buy. But, from within the dirt and rocks is where the gems themselves are born and hide. So, is this not a fitting place?"

Luna just shrugged.

"How much do you think you know about the matter of Pacific Splendor, Luna?"

"You salted a riverbed on The Big Island with a diamond and then fooled the insurance company, the jewelry industry, and the world press into thinking it was the gemological find of the century. And you arranged the sinking of *The Shilpa* so that you could, among other things, swindle Safe Pacific out of $15 million. To quote Miguel, "It was a goddamned brilliant plan.""

"That is very good thinking, Luna! But, you still don't know what I *really* intend to do,"

"Does it have something to do with that cricket bag I saw in your hotel room?"

Rupee nodded. "I fooled you into believing that Mr. Stone, my Maori bodyguard behind you, was an A.L.O.H.A. operative."

"*Maori?*" Luna asked.

"A native of New Zealand who *looks like* a Hawaiian—a useful souvenir I picked up in Australia, and then fixed up with falsified Indian credentials. He passed *Shilpa's* security and was permitted to board. It was Stone who chased us to my suite. Inside, you pretended to love me. Your kisses, though good, were trickeries, Luna; you really cared only for finding the diamond."

"Your love-making was just as laughable, Rupee," Luna sniped. "As for "*The Shilpa's* security," Alsia Aapt itemized and verified the safe's contents. If Pacific Splendor was deposited in the safe, and the safe was never opened until after salvage, it should have been there. So, Alsia lied about your deposit, or maybe she removed Pacific Splendor during the sinking. But either way, all you have now is a worthless hot rock, instead of a near priceless piece of ice."

"I cannot payoff everyone. Someone would, in due course, have discovered Pacific Splendor's falsity. The diamond has served its purpose, Luna. Now, I shall show you something of greater value." Rupee snapped his fingers. Miguel Diamante stepped from behind Luna and disappeared into the den. When he emerged from the shadows, it was with Rupee's cricket bag. Miguel sat it down and stepped aside. Rupee bent over, unzipped the bag, and pulled out a heavy, metal canister with a yellow handle on top. "This is fissionable material," Rupee announced.

The lead from the bag sample! Luna realized too late. "So that's where your millions from playing cricket go, and why you gambled for more!" she deduced.

"I gambled to be seen—an Ali Baba, as you say, Luna."

"An *alibi*, you mean," Luna corrected Rupee. "But the reference to Ali Baba is apropos, I guess, since you could qualify as one of "the 40 thieves.""

Rupee chuckled. "Anyway," he continued, "the true risk was to involve many people in my plan. Most of them are not people of vision; they cannot see past today. So, I had to pay them for their parts to play. Miguel's acquaintances at I.C.E. made it easy to buy their certification. Then I funded, shall we say, a scientist to post his gemological judgments online. I paid Miguel to claim to be a movie maker and trick a bum from the slums to drive a boat to the set, *Shilpa,* I mean."

"Not a Tony-winning performance, but better pay than Broadway!" Diamante said.

Rupee continued. "I paid *Shilpa's* engineer to play cricket, not to attend to the engines. Then, Stone disposes of the engineer; your coastal patrol destroys the bum; *Shilpa* sinks; and at last, because of your tradition of open borders to all, I slipped in my fissionable material before the routine coastal patrol inspection could discover it."

"And who's the prime sinking suspect? A.L.O.H.A. is—*what a plan!*" Luna said.

"But I "plan" to make millions more, Luna. I read that centuries ago the British arrived here and thought they found diamonds. Thus, they named one of Hawaii's most famous volcanoes "Diamond Head." But what the British found were worthless calcite crystals. Yet the belief that diamonds can be found near volcanoes has been proven to be scientifically sound and valuable.

"Perhaps your new useful lover, Lono, has told you of this. But, with his tongue likely in your ear, perhaps it is worth repeating that it takes tremendous pressure to create diamonds, and then the awesome force of volcanic eruptions to bring them near the surface. Hawaii has some extinct volcanoes that may have countless diamonds trapped below them. The millions from my cricket playing and what was gained by Pacific Splendor's publicity have given me the method by which to release these diamonds, or to perhaps even create more diamonds of size."

Luna finally realized Rupee's true intentions. "You're going to explode a nuke under a volcano—*Jesus, Rupee!*" she gasped.

"I prefer Vishnu, but yes: It is a god-like inspiration," Rupee replied.

Luna tried to argue, "But the damage from the blast..,"

"Temporary," Rupee interrupted. "It can be explained as the result of another earthquake, in a land filled with them."

"And what about the radiation?"

At first, Rupee's tone was regretful. "Yes, a shame," he sighed. Then he smiled, as his grand design blossomed. "But, it is necessary. And, it shall be blamed on A.L.O.H.A. terrorism. When it is safe to do so, I shall return to the excavation site for the diamonds."

"In what, a thousand years?!" Luna laughed at the notion. "With the half-life of the radiation..."

"It didn't take "a thousand years" to restore Hiroshima, did it Luna? Nor shall it now. When I recover and make known my discoveries, they shall rebuild the island, giving it a new mining industry; its people, money and jobs; and their children, vision and security. Pacific Splendor shall again be a true reality, Luna, not just the name of a transplanted, altered diamond. "

"What do you want from me, Rupee?" the insurance investigator finally asked.

"Your allegiance, not hindrance," Rupee responded. "I did not have you killed at the hotel or in Nani's car for a reason, Luna: It is because I like your style. Not just your clothes, but how you think; and, from the way you handled the corrupt farmers, your strength. Having a smart, strong, and beautiful woman presents many advantages. So please, join my team."

Luna advised, "My commission is 3 percent of the value of the diamond. But, I'll cut you a deal: Make it $100,000—a signing bonus, in keeping with sports metaphors. First, I need to issue a report to the insurer that Pacific Splendor is lost and that it's okay for them to accept your claim. Then, I'll need to bribe—I mean, convince—others to forget looking into this any further."

Rupee moaned, "And then, you shall require a new wardrobe; and then, make-up..."

"How else can a girl keep up the "beautiful" side of the bargain?"

"And I thought you to be less greedy than most women," Rupee sighed. He pressed a finger to his lips and thought. "I shall make you a counter proposal: You can either accept $10,000 or..."

Stone grabbed Luna and wrapped her in a choke

hold. Rupee continued to say, "...or, like Nani Nyoko and *Shilpa's* engineers, you can be the victim of an unfortunate *accident*."

"You leave me no choice, Rupee," Luna rasped. "Ten thousand it is."

Rupee snapped his fingers, and Stone released Luna. She rubbed feeling back into her neck and reached for her pocket. But, the insurance investigator stopped when she felt Stone's gun (again pressed into her back).

Rupee gripped his armrests. "What are you reaching for, Luna?" he demanded to know.

"Something that you may find useful: My smartphone," she calmly replied.

"That's right!" Miguel Diamante chimed-in. "Nani told me that Nightcrow keeps a lot of data on that phone."

"For instance, I have the geological report from the company that led me to look into whether Pacific Splendor was real," Luna said. "With my phone, I can download it from my laptop. Then, I can get you my laptop."

Rupee's eyebrows rose. "Maybe this shall earn you the money you seek." Then, he snapped his fingers and said, "Mister Stone, the phone please!"

Stone shoved his gun into his doctor's overcoat and stepped in front of Luna. With Rupee's permission, she reached into her front pocket and meekly removed her smartphone. Stone snatched it, smirked, and then turned to take it to his boss. All Luna could do was watch Stone … *watch Stone!* She saw just the back of the bodyguard's formidable frame, not Rupee and Miguel. That meant they couldn't see around him either; they couldn't look at Luna. But it wouldn't last.

Now's my chance! Luna thought. According to plan, she grabbed the Doro 410 cellphone from her hip pocket, flipped it open, and speed-dialed her smartphone number. Instantly, it rang. Stone stopped a few feet from Rupee, reflexively pressed "answer," and then … *ZAP!*

With a shower of sparks and puff of white smoke, 60,000 volts shot from the overloaded Yellow Jacket smartphone stun gun case. Stone took the brunt of the electric blow; he shook and crumbled into a groaning heap on the ground. Miguel shrieked from the burning flash and fought to regain sight. Rupee jumped up and bowled his chair at Luna. She ducked and dived for the gun that shook free from Stone. Miguel Diamante reached under his polo shirt for a real handgun. But Luna was faster on the draw, releasing a rapid burst of tranquilizer shots that flew into Miguel's leg and stomach. The gemologist got off one shot, but it missed Luna. His hands began to feel heavy and tingly; then, his eyes fluttered wildly; and finally, the gun fell to the ground. Miguel's limp frame followed, and Luna ran over and grabbed the gun. *"Curtains!"* she spat at the former thespian.

Luna then looked for the cricket bag, but it and Rupee were both gone. She ran for the stairs. Halfway down, the sight of smoke clouds along the gravel road leading up to the house caught Luna's attention. The sound of sirens pierced the air, as six police cars roared up. Two stopped and blocked the driveway leading out to the road, while the rest surrounded Miguel Diamante's sedan in the distance. Luna suddenly saw Lono and Detective Sergeant Valerosa appear. But, she also saw everyone setting up for a fight. Not wanting to be mistaken for a bad guy and shot, Luna took off her white T-shirt and waved it (as she crossed the open field for safety). She heard someone shout, "Hold your fire!" *It worked!* Wonder if it would if I were 93, instead of 43? Luna couldn't help but to think. Probably not: They might shoot to put me out of my misery!

At a few yards away, Luna put her shirt back on and ducked behind Valerosa's car.

The Detective Sergeant asked, "Are you okay, Ms. Nightcrow? I mean, *mentally* okay?!"

"Sorry for the striptease," Luna panted, "but I forgot my supply of white flags."

"You could always text your terms of surrender, you know!" Lono laughed. "I waited almost an hour outside the hospital, before I figured something was up. So, I turned on the GPS location tracking link to your smartphone. It worked like a charm, and I called in the police."

Luna finally caught her breath. "Rupee Sabal is holed up somewhere on the top floor. I took down Miguel Diamante and Rupee's bodyguard."

Lono grinned. *"Damn, girl!"*

"But, Rupee's got a nuclear core with him."

Lono's jaw dropped. *"What the...?!"*

"A bomb?" Valerosa asked, but more discreetly.

"It's not a bomb, but the fuel for one. You know, plutonium, uranium? It won't blow, but could still cause contamination," Luna said.

Two of the driveway officers knocked on the front door. Valerosa pulled a bullhorn from her car. "Rupert Sabal, this's Detective Sergeant Valerosa of the Honolulu Police Department. We want to talk to you. Please, show yourself." There was no reaction from either level of the old, gray compound. "Rupert Sabal, please show yourself. You have my word that you will not be harmed!"

CHAPTER 25

Hot Pursuit

Suddenly, there was a response: A roar. Then, from the ground floor, a cargo van blasted through what was a garage door. Police officers blocking the driveway dove for cover as the dark gray van smashed into their cruisers. Rupee hit the reverse and pulled away from the wreck. The other officers surrounding the sedan immediately rushed for the house, but were still out of range for effective handgun fire.

When the first shots rang out from the driveway cops, Rupee grinned. "Like kids throwing rocks!" he thought, hearing a few bullets splatter, but not penetrate, the armored hull.

Rupee geared up. The van's massive push bar bulldozed one of crumpled cruisers aside—enough to give Rupee an opening. Quickly, he shifted gears again, sped up, and rumbled up the driveway, and down the open road in a cloud of dust. The haze made accurate return fire futile, for now. But the police would get another shot, as Detective Sergeant Valerosa jumped into her Crown Vic squad car. Luna barely got inside, closing the door as the wheels spun and spit gravel. The two women raced away in hot pursuit of Rupee and his perilous payload.

"Where the hell are we?" Luna asked.

"Diamond Head Crater," Valerosa answered.

"Inside of it?!"

"Not anymore. We're going down one of the slopes." Valerosa then yanked up her police radio receiver and issued an all units response.

The rock-strewn volcano road led the squad car on a dangerous, downhill drop that finally twisted and turned into forested, suburban lowlands. All of a sudden, a stop sign appeared. But with tangled timbers obscuring a clear view of the flow of traffic on the road beyond, Valerosa had to stop. When she determined it was safe, the Detective Sergeant turned left onto what was a two-lane highway that hugged the slopes. On the other side of the guard rail and dozens of feet below stretched the vast Pacific Ocean. The siren and lights swiped traffic to the side, allowing Valerosa and Luna to make up for lost time. Suddenly, the police radio buzzed. There was a report of a cargo van in the vicinity.

"It's near Light House Road?" Valerosa asked for confirmation.

When dispatch confirmed, Valerosa hit the brakes

and twirled a U-turn. The squad car took off in the opposite direction and didn't stop, until it reached a small, red-and-white-colored light house state park off the highway. And parked on the road that led to the historic marker and small picnic area was a battered, gray cargo van with a blown back tire.

Valerosa brought the squad car to a screeching halt. She drew her Smith & Wesson 9 MM pistol and got out. Luna followed, but Valerosa signaled for her to stay back. The Detective Sergeant moved swiftly toward the van. Once there, she and peeked through the driver's side window. No one was inside. Then, Valerosa proceeded to search around and below the van.

Meanwhile, Luna decided to try the light house. She crept down the narrow dirt path to the cliff on which the old structure stood. Once there, she noticed that the door was ajar. The insurance investigator drew the Browning semi-automatic handgun from her back pocket. She pushed the door open and stepped inside. The bottom floor was empty. Luna looked up the spiral staircase, but saw no one at the top. Maybe Rupee's hiding behind the beacon, she thought.

Quietly, Luna climbed the stairs. She reached the top and swung her gun around the renovated beacon that capped the platform. Then she inched her head in for a look. But, no one was there. The platform did provide a great view of the ocean. So

174

Luna eased up and watched the boats and parasails play in the Pacific, wishing that she could be out there on one of them. But her reverie was rudely interrupted by the sound of sirens. Luna sighed and hurried downstairs.

Police backup was on the scene and cordoned off the area. Luna approached Valerosa. "Nothing in the light house," she said. "What about the van: Did you find the core?"

"If it's in there, then it's someone else's party," the Detective Sergeant replied almost happily. "Hazmat and the bomb squad are on their way. We have an APB for Sabal and you can bet the feds and the military will be on him, too."

Suddenly, something about Rupee's plan occurred to Luna. She automatically reached for her smartphone, but remembered that she fried it. So, Luna took out her standby Doro 410 and dialed. "Hello, Lono?" she said.

"Luna," he answered, "you okay?"

"Yeah," she replied. "How about you?"

"I'm still up at Sabal's hideout," Lono responded. "The cops arrested Diamante and the bodyguard, but they haven't found that nuclear fuel."

"Rupee's on the run with it," Luna said.

"Do you know where to, Luna?"

"Maybe," she told Lono.

CHAPTER 26

Once More Unto the Breach

An ordinary produce truck travelled down the southeastern stretches of the coastal highway leading out of Honolulu. It then pulled off the road. The driver left the cab and went to the back of the truck. He quickly rolled it open. Rupee Sabal poked his head up from behind the crates of fruits and vegetables. The driver motioned for him to come out. Rupee got his cricket bag and climbed down. He unzipped the bag and produced a white envelope. The driver opened it and quickly thumbed through over a dozen one hundred dollar bills. He shook Rupee's hand and returned to the cab. The truck started, and Rupee watched it drive out of sight. He slung his cricket bag and hurried across the highway. Then, he carefully descended the steep, grassy bank that led to the rocky shoreline below.

Rupee looked at his watch. And, right on schedule, he saw a high speed inflatable motor boat appear. It got closer and closer, until it buzzed onto the beach. The lone Asian crewman signaled for Rupee to climb in. Once aboard, the motor started and the boat travelled to a spot about 12 miles out. Rupee soon saw a gray cone sticking up from the water. Then, the water turned black and rolled off the length of a surfacing midget sub. The hatch opened and a short man in a white naval officer's uniform climbed through. He helped Rupee off the boat. Neither spoke the other's language. So, both spoke English.

"Once more unto the breach...?" the Korean laughed.

"Yes.., dear friend," Rupee confirmed. "*Henry V* was never my favorite Shakespeare play to read in school. But, the quotation is indeed appropriate, Captain Dong-Min."

Rupee handed Dong-Min the cricket bag and then fitted himself through the hatch. Dong-Min relayed orders to the motorboat crewman and disappeared below. The crewman took a machete and hacked a hole in the bottom of the boat. Water began to bubble up. The crewman climbed off and into the midget sub, securing the hatch behind him. The inflatable boat and the midget sub quickly vanished below the waves.

Dong-Min told his lone crewman to take the controls. The captain then walked through the small, cigar-shaped cabin to where Rupee was. Rupee struggled to settle into a comfortable position. "This is not *The Shilpa*," Dong-Min said with a grin.

"Let us hope not!" Rupee grunted.

"You should have let me torpedo it."

"*And start World War 3?!* No. This way, the Americans and Indians do not know what happened. They are investigating many possibilities that will distract attention and resources away from my plans."

"I only meant that at a maximum near the surface speed of 12 knots, we still will not arrive at Kailua-Kona Pier for approximately 18 hours."

Rupee finally found a position that allowed him to at least unzip his cricket bag. "In your part of the world, there is a saying: "The wise man adapts himself to circumstances, as water shapes itself to the vessel that contains it," Rupee said, handing Dong-Min a thick manila envelope. "And that contains payment not for comfort, but for *safe* passage."

The captain took the envelope; and then, a seat. "Departure from Oahu will be safe enough," he told Rupee. "Current reports are that the Honolulu police are conducting a ground search, while the American and Indian militaries are searching air and port terminals on Maui and Oahu. In the remote chance that we are detected, the outer design of this vessel closely resembles that of several pleasure submarines in the area. We will be regarded as tourists and ignored."

"What about travelling the open sea?"

"The American navy is busy with the salvage of *The Shilpa* and their normal duties."

"Duties that are normally meant to catch their enemies," Rupee warned.

"I have mapped a route that takes us through the shallowest depths possible, where sonar readings take time to distinguish from sea life and geological formations," Dong-Min replied. "But, if we are to dive to retrieve your parcel, we will have to travel below the water for part of the journey. That reduces our speed to 8 knots, and may delay arrival by about 2 hours."

"What of the parcel?" Rupee asked anxiously. "With its recipient likely in custody, did...?"

The captain nodded. "The courier from Panna jettisoned it in a low acoustic metal case, as you instructed, to prevent American Customs detection," he replied. "Our obstacle avoidance sonar will lock onto its homing signal. And, the robot arm will retrieve it."

"Captain Dong-Min, it seems as though you have thought of everything."

The cricketer stretched out along the wall and folded his hands peacefully on his lap. Suddenly, a beeping noise sent fright flowing through Rupee. Captain Dong-Min turned and rushed toward to the helm. Rupee stood, grabbed onto the overhead hand rails, and followed.

Dong-Min's crewman relayed something in

Korean; and, to Rupee, the tone sounded troublesome. The Captain took the controls. He studied the sonar screen, finding the lone blip he was alerted to. Dong-Min told his crewman to man the radio console, while he took the helm. After a minute, the overhead speaker fizzed to life. And the voice on the other end spoke English.

"Poseidon to Olympus...unidentified bogie..." The voice cut out, lost in a sea of static.

The American Navy! Rupee's heart fluttered at the thought. Then, it heaved towards his throat, as the cricketer felt a bump and a rising sensation. But when Rupee looked at Dong-Min, he saw no hesitation. Not a twitch, not a sound, just steely composure as he raised the wheel.

If we're surfacing, we'll be seen! Rupee thought. But the sub remained on course. *He's betrayed me!* Before the panicked charge escaped Rupee's lips, the American voice returned over the radio. "Olympus, sonar reading was negative, repeat negative. It must have been a whale calf."

The crewman sighed. And Captain Dong-Min turned to Rupee with a smug smile.

After a moment, Rupee's nerves ease off enough for a chuckle. "You have proven your point, captain," he admitted. "I was wrong to doubt you. This shall be a safe trip, indeed!"

CHAPTER 27

Scene of the Next Crime

Luna caught an online replay of the evening news. The broadcast's continuing coverage of the missing diamond led off. This time, it was with reports of a run on metal detectors and increases in charter boat and scuba business. Various experts, however, appeared to emphasize the danger in amateurs trying to recover Pacific Splendor from the ocean. Luna wasn't surprised that the arrests of Nani, Miguel, and Stone weren't mentioned (not with all that was at stake). But, there was an interesting interview with another player in the Diamond Head deception: Ailani Haku.

The A.L.O.H.A. leader deflected the anchorwoman's attempts to turn the interview into a heated debate over Hawaiian secession. Instead, Alani revealed that A.L.O.H.A. had what would prove to be "troubling knowledge of a major crime committed against the Autonomous Land." She then announced that the group was working with law enforcement and independent investigators to "apprehend the wrongdoers."

When the anchorwoman asked for more specifics, Ailani replied, "Isn't that what your reporters are paid to gather? Or is it just dust, in this age where everyone's cellphone cameras can make them a reporter or even an anchorwoman?" On that note, the interview ended abruptly.

Luna smiled. *"Ole Ailani played them like a water drum!"* she laughed. Suddenly, Luna's cellphone rang. And the number displayed on the Caller ID made the insurance investigator's stomach flip and toes tap. It was the one man she most wanted to hear from...*for the moment, anyway.* "Aloha, Lieutenant Bay," Luna answered. "Well, what did you come up with?"

"We really appreciate your sharing the tip you received, Ms. Nightcrow. But, Customs didn't find the shipment of $50,000 in diamonds that was scheduled to arrive last night," Lieutenant Bay confirmed.

Dammit! Luna seethed to herself. She quickly played her other hunch, hoping for better results. "What about the river valley on Hawaii?" she asked.

"The authorities in Hilo have it staked out and some geologists from the local university are scheduled to survey it later this morning. But, so far, no sign of Sabal or diamonds in that area either. The feds are even re-tasking their Pacific satellites to aid in the search."

"Please keep an eye out for Alsia Aapt, *The Shilpa's* head of security. She's from Panna, India: The area from where the diamonds were exported. That's not a crime, but I'm certain that she's involved in the whole deal. She could be on the run with Rupee, or maybe murdered."

"Do you know if the Honolulu PD has any leads from Sabal's other accomplices?" Bay asked.

"It looks like the police didn't release the news, but Nani Nyoko, Miguel Diamante, and Rupee's bodyguard are all in custody. When I last talked with Detective Sergeant Valerosa, she said the suspects are sticking to the claim that they didn't know about nuclear material being smuggled in. Nani told the police that controlled use of radiation to change the color of gems is standard practice."

"Which may give Sabal a defense, if the nuclear material is tied to him," Bay noted.

"He's still looking at kidnapping, bribery, being an accomplice to murder, and sundry other sins," Luna counteracted.

She heard the Lieutenant chuckle, "Of course, Ms. Nightcrow."

"Anyhow, the police are supposed to keep me posted. You're a bigger fish than me, though, and will most likely get the line on any new PD leads first," Luna said.

"Well, everybody's doing their best. So thank you again, Ms. Nightcrow."

"Good luck, Lieutenant."

"To us all," Bay replied.

The cellular line dropped off and Luna felt a headache coming on. She shrank into the soft living room couch, but not at Nani's house. After several hours of debriefing by the Honolulu PD, very interested representatives of Sagar Excursions, and a federal agent or two, Luna spent the night at Lono's Gold Coast beach house, but not sleeping. Before Lieutenant Bay called, she was engaged in more Web browsing. But now, the insurance investigator closed her laptop, trudged out of the living room, and went outside. Luna shivered. The Pacific Ocean's breeze was enlivening; and the relentless crash of its white breakers onto the blue-black shores beyond, exhilarating.

Meanwhile, Lono rolled out of an empty bed. It was still dark outside the bedroom window. He yawned and ran his fingers through his hair, trying to shake the remaining sleepiness from his head. He then threw on a T-shirt and shorts and stopped by the kitchen. Lono saw Luna through the sliding door, sprinkled in silver moonlight and wearing the guest kimono he loaned her—*and wearing it well!* A few minutes later, he dared to approach her. "Good morning," Lono said softly, with a cup of hot Kona in his hand.

Luna turned around. "Good for Rupee, maybe," she grunted. After a moment, she apologized. Luna then noticed the coffee and asked, *"For me?"*

"For me," Lono said. "You're wired enough!" Lono gave Luna a rascally grin, then the cup.

But Luna couldn't drink. "I just got off the phone with the Coast Guard," she moaned.

"No diamonds," Lono stated the obvious. "Well, maybe the tip-off about the diamonds was bogus, a trick to throw us off Sabal's trail."

"No, it's legit. A.L.O.H.A.'s leader gave it to me. As a matter of fact, if you can believe it, she turned over a new leaf on the news last night and is now helping the cops look for Rupee!"

"What people will do to save their ass," Lono chuckled. "And now that nothing turned up, A.L.O.H.A. is going to look like bigger asses than they are!"

"Maybe not," Luna said. "It looks like the courier got word of Diamante's arrest. Maybe he kept the diamonds for himself. But Rupee knew about the arrests for sure. He might still have use for the diamonds as payoffs, now that the salting is over. But maybe…"

"But nothing: The con is kaput!" Lono butt in. "Your insurance company won't have to pay-out and you get a payday. *So relax!* Let the cops, the feds, and their new A.L.O.H.A. *friends* find the nuclear fuel."

"How can you be so casual about this?" Luna

huffed. "Rupee rigged this scam so that I would look for Pacific Splendor and not the nuclear material."

"You said it yourself, Luna: It's not a bomb!" Lono shot back. "Now, drink your Kona before it gets cold."

At that moment, Luna's eyes widened and the coffee cup fell from her hand onto the deck.

Lono shrugged. "Okay, then don't drink it," he said, heading into the house.

"*Kona coffee!*" Luna thought aloud. "Lono, is Kona the town it comes from?"

"The *area* it comes from," he clarified. "Kai-lua-Kona's the town: A sleepy little cruise ship port on the west side of The Big Island…so what, Luna?"

"Rupee planned to use the fuel to—Lono, we've got to get to Hawaii…*now!*"

"*What for?* The cops are already looking through the river valley where the salting was."

"But that's not where Rupee's headed," Luna said.

Lono gave-in. "Then where are we headed?" he sighed.

"To the scene of the next crime," Luna replied.

CHAPTER 28

The Cover of Darkness

A periscope broke the surface of the ocean. Topside, it was dark. Up the coast, Captain Dong-Min saw a cruise ship tucked into its berth. And it seemed that Kailua-Kona's 10,000 or so residents were also tucked in for the night. The only things that were awake were the street lights. It was just what Rupee Sabal hoped for.

Dong-Min carefully guided the midget sub into the bay and surfaced. The hatch opened and out popped Rupee and his cricket bag. Rupee stood and slung the bag over his shoulder. Then, he climbed up the pier's rock sea wall and onto the dock. Dong-Min submerged and Rupee continued on (under the cover of pre-dawn darkness).

After taking a moment to rest his tired arms and legs, Rupee started out for the main street along the ocean front. There was no traffic, so he crossed easily. After a 10-mintue walk inland, Rupee arrived at an old Quonset hut on the edge of the brush. He went to the door, knocked three times, and waited. The door creaked open to a crack. A set of dark eyes barely stuck out and looked him over suspiciously. Rupee said something that soon erased the door-woman's suspicions. The door opened and Rupee walked into the embrace of a short, stocky woman. *"Rupee!"* Alsia sighed. "It is truly you! You are all right?"

Rupee grinned. "I am," he answered. Rupee then looked deeply into Alsia's gray eyes. "You do not have to continue with us, Alsia. It may still be dangerous."

"I was in charge of securing an entire ocean vessel, Rupee!" Alsia laughed. But then, her laugher turned to a moment of sadness. "But now, I cannot guar-antee my own security."

"Nor can I," Rupee admitted.

"The diamond is worthless. I have no ship, no salary—only this job to do. I will stay."

Rupee rewarded Alsia with a kiss on her fore-head. And, on tip-toes, she was able to give him a peck on the cheek. The former head of security then escorted Rupee to a regular-looking pickup truck and a motorcycle in the middle of the hut. Alsia sailed one last smile Rupee's way and then left to join 2 other men in loading machinery onto the truck's flat bed. Rupee looked for one other person. He found him at the back of the hut, hunched over a workbench that was illuminated by a work light.

Rupee walked over to the bald old man in a white lab coat and tapped him on the shoulder. The old man turned from working on a circuit board. Rupee unzipped his cricket bag and presented him with the heavy, gray canister and a black, metal container with a small key taped on top. The old man sat the canister aside and picked up the black box. He untaped the key, inserted it into the lock, and turned it. The lid rose; and with it, the old man's glasses. He inspected the contents: A pile of small, clear stones. When the old man held them to the work light, they sparkled and winked 50,000 times at him. He suddenly felt much younger, in the presence of such beauty and the possibility it presented. *"Perfect!"* he said, returning his glasses to the bridge of his nose.

Rupee grinned. "Is it not better payment than you once received for grading papers and preparing dry lectures, Professor Sudhir?" he asked.

The old man nodded.

Then, Rupee became serious. "You have your final payment," he said. "Now, professor, how much longer have you to finish the bomb?"

CHAPTER 29

The Road to Riches

The sun finally rolled back the cover of darkness, and orange dawn stretched across the sky. Thirty minutes later, Lono Kuhl's pilot prepared the twin engine Piper Mojave for an early morning trip to Kona International Airport on The Big Island.

Luna was too nervous to eat, but Lono finished off a hearty breakfast of *loco moco* (shrimp, dolphinfish, and rice topped with a fried egg), Kona, and a side of *poi* (a vegetable liquid). "So," he said, wiping his mouth, "you still think Sabal's headed for The Big Island to nuke for diamonds?"

"Yes," Luna sighed.

"I thought you said that Diamond Head was the target."

"Rupee first picked Diamond Head because it's an extinct volcano. He may have just been surveying it, but the plan failed. So, which island has the most volcanoes? Hawaii. And which of its volcanoes is the oldest and extinct? Kohala is. He also mentioned "giving the island a new industry": Making it wealthy, in other words. From what I've seen of Greater Honolulu, Oahu isn't the island hurting for more money and status."

"Hawaii is economically poorer than Oahu and mostly rural," Lono said. Then, he nodded in full agreement. "It all makes sense. Sabal could also blend-in with the other Kailua-Kona tourists, unless there are cricket fans around, which isn't likely. And Kohala Volcano is only a little over an hour's drive north. But how do we know that he didn't set everything up, press the timer, and then leave? We could be walking into a trap, Luna."

"Yeah," she confessed. "But I'm guessing that Rupee probably took a boat here, to avoid tighter airport security. If so, it's about 200 miles from Oahu to Hawaii; that's nearly a day's trip. Rupee escaped yesterday afternoon. So, depending on how fast the boat went, he should either have just arrived or isn't too far from getting there. And, if the diamond courier dropped off the diamonds and bomb-making materials before arriving in Honolulu, the bomb may not be fully built. Remember, Rupee only had the core with him. As for "a trap," I doubt it. Rupee probably thinks we're still focused on Diamond Head, not backwater Kohala."

"All that hassle, when Sabal could have made more diamonds in a lab!" Lono laughed.

"Pacific Splendor's a lab creation; and look what it got him," Luna said.

"Almost a $15 million payout, for a kind of amateurish design," Lono answered. "When done with the right equipment and technicians, Luna, it's hard to tell the difference between lab-created diamonds and real ones. I mean, they take basically the same materials that real diamonds are made from and configure new ones. The lab creations have virtually the same chemical and visual qualities as the real deal."

"But there is a big difference, Lono: Perception. Man-made vs. natural means a huge price difference. And if lab diamonds start flooding the market as "real," then there could be considerable overpayment on claims," Luna argued.

"You know, for all the fuss over Pacific Splendor, it's a blip on the natural resource radar. Hawaii's sources of geothermal energy are much bigger assets—*hundreds of times bigger!*" Lono added. "When I talked to Sabal, he seemed like a cool guy. Cool enough to maybe join Gems of the Rim as a spokesman or something and open up more of the Indian market. Whatever made him go nuts and try nuking for diamonds anyway?"

"Maybe we did," Luna replied.

"*What?!*"

"Not *we*, as in you and me, but the U.S. government.

Last night, I did some more digging online and ran across a since-cancelled Cold War program called Operation Plowshare. The U.S. and the U.S.S.R. researched peaceful uses for nuclear weapons, Lono. One of the proposed uses was for, believe it or not, mapping and excavating ores."

Lono leaned back in his chair. "Luna," he said, "you've thought of everything."

"Semper Paratus," she replied.

Lono threw up his hands. "Just when everything made sense, you lost me again!"

The plane finally took off. A half an hour later, it landed at a private hangar at Kona International. Luna and Lono left the plane but didn't get far. A convoy of white cars roared to a halt inside the hangar bay. Several tough-looking men got out and made a bee-line for them.

The men's uniforms and the vehicles' flashing lights and wailing sirens calmed Luna, but not Lono. He lobbed Luna a nervous glance. "You're sure that "Plowshare" thing you looked up online last night was declassified, right?" he asked.

Rupee Sabal was amazed by the scenery that whizzed by, as his pickup truck (packed with terrifying freight) and a motorcycle escort climbed the mountain roads to Kohala Volcano. Tree-lined stretches and picturesque pastures of peacefully-grazing cattle and sheep passed. Clouds covered the horizon, but the sky began to break into blue. Once the clouds dissolved into a passing mist, the ominous appearance of two distinct cinder cones snapped Rupee back to the reality of what lay ahead.

"We dug a hole into the volcano's surface," the old man, whom Rupee called "Professor Sudhir," said. "About 2 miles was as far as we could hollow out."

Rupee sighed. "Two miles is approximately the depth of most of the islands' other volcanic pipes," he said. "I hoped to set off the bomb much deeper."

"But, an explosion at 2 miles will make everything seem natural. Besides, we deposited many large sacks of graphite at various sites within the crater. This will assist in creating diamonds, should the volcano lack natural ones," Professor Sudhir explained.

"*Ingenious!*" Rupee marveled.

"I am sorry that I could not get a second bomb created for use as the A.L.O.H.A. weapon."

"One is enough. A.L.O.H.A. shall still be to blame. What strength is the bomb, professor?"

"Sixteen kilotons: That is a little less than the Nagasaki bomb."

Professor Sudhir thought. "Rupee, if this does not work, I've been thinking …"

"You should "think" more positively, Professor, for it shall work," Rupee interrupted. He then laughed. "But thinking is your nature; so, proceed."

"We should try for diamonds in Antarctica next. It has the most volcanoes on earth," Professor Sudhir suggested.

Rupee recoiled at the idea. "The diamonds may not crack from the cold, but I surely would!

As the curved, two-lane highway finally straightened out into one long black thread, it reminded Rupee a bit of a line of gunpowder leading from a powder keg. And soon, the match would be struck. And, with some luck, diamonds would burst from centuries of encrusted captivity and be cut by jewelers into all forms of dazzling creativity.

As the pick-up motored along, Rupee's dreams of diamonds led him to think that he saw other gems. Rubies and sapphires dotted the distance. But as the truck moved closer, the gemstones turned into an all-too familiar sight—emergency lights. The road to riches was blocked off! *Damn!* The truck driver saw the sheriff and police departments' barricade and roared to a halt. The motorcyclist swerved to avoid a collision. The truck backed up, wheeled across both lanes, and turned in the other direction. The motorcyclist followed, as the sound of sirens filled the air. And, from the air, a police helicopter dropped in altitude to chase the pickup down the mountain too.

Meanwhile, Luna and Lono hung on for dear life as the speedometer on the sheriff's cruiser they rode in was off the chart. The sheriff looked over his shoulder to Luna in the back seat. "If we knock the truck off the road, will the material blow?" he asked.

"The fuel won't. If it's been put into a bomb, it still has to be armed to explode," Luna answered.

"And if that's Sabal, his target's the volcano; so, he probably didn't arm it yet," Lono added his two cents for reassurance.

The sheriff issued new orders over the radio to the lead cruiser. It increased speed and caught up to the pickup. Rupee saw the deputy cruiser through the side mirror and really began to sweat. The deputy at the wheel edged toward the back bumper, preparing to steer the truck off the road. But then, Rupee heard a familiar buzz that he hopped was the sound of salvation. It was the motorcyclist. The motorcycle veered into the oncoming traffic lane, sending cars screeching to a halt or swerving to the side. The motorcycle finally pulled alongside the deputy cruiser. But, the rider saw that there was still space between the truck and cruiser. The motorcycle suddenly weaved for the tight space. It was suicide.

The deputy cruiser slammed into the motorcycle's back tire, turning it into its line of travel and crushing the rider underneath. The cruiser bucked and careened toward the side of the road. The deputy lost control of the steering, overshot the shoulder, and rumbled downhill into a grassy ditch.

Rupee's eyes closed and his head dropped. The word "Alsia" parted his lips. Motorcyclist Alsia

Aapt's quick-thinking increased their chances of escape, just as it had previously allowed him to stall Luna Nightcrow's investigation (by taking out the engine room worker and an unreliable ally in Nani Nyoko). But the sight ahead gave Rupee little time to mourn.

The landscape was lethal, switching back to winding, narrow passes with an increase in oncoming traffic. But, the pickup truck driver poured on the gas. He knew that the remaining cruisers would play it safe and slow down. They had the advantage of the helicopter to match or exceed the pickup's speed. Rupee turned and banged on the cab back window, alerting the pickup's fourth passenger in the flat bed.

The man in the flat bed previously had but one job: To guard the bomb. But with Alsia gone, he had to protect the rear, too. The man wobbled to a steady position. His hands raised a long metal tube to his shoulders. Fixed to the front was a rocket. The man could feel the pickup slow, trying to give him a steady aim at the helicopter (and a shot at evening the odds).

But Luna saw what was happening. *"Oh, shit! Sheriff!"* she cried.

The sheriff saw the rocket and grabbed his radio receiver to alert the helicopter pilot. The message got through and the helicopter broke off pursuit. The flat bed passenger crouched down, but he gave the pickup what it needed: A manageable 2 on 1 chase. But, as soon as the road straightened, the sheriff increased speed again. Like the ditched deputy cruiser had tried to do, the sheriff prepared to get into position to turn the pickup off the road. But instead, he slid into the left-hand lane. The passenger side window rolled down, and the deputy riding shotgun stuck one out. He took deadly aim at the back tire and fired. It burst, causing the pickup driver to lose control. The truck swerved and almost spun 360 degrees. But, it crashed into the guard rail and came to rest at almost across the road. The driver's side was smashed. The flat bed passenger was thrown from the wreck and plastered across the pavement.

The helicopter sat down a few yards behind the wrecked pickup. And when its passenger door opened, out jumped an Asian woman in civilian clothes with a Geiger counter slung over her shoulder. She ignited two road flares (to warn oncoming traffic) and proceeded to the back of the pickup. Coming down the road, the two pursuing sheriff's cruisers jammed on the brakes and blocked the front of the pickup. Luna and Lono, along with the sheriff and his deputies, poured out.

Meanwhile, inside the pickup, the driver's face was buried in the steering wheel; his neck was broken. Professor Sudhir leaned on his shoulder, with blood streaming from a massive head wound. Rupee's head was the only one that moved. It rose slowly, but it hurt to focus his eyes. He looked through the cracked windshield and saw a deputy moving toward the truck. Rupee knew he was out of luck.

The pickup's passenger side door banged open. Rupee tumbled out with a pistol. He staggered to his feet and headed towards the back of the truck. Startled, the Asian woman inside stopped inspecting the bomb.

An approaching deputy shouted, "Stop," but Rupee didn't. He turned and yelled something in Hindi at the deputy. The officer only saw the pistol and opened fire. Rupee's left arm took a hit, but he didn't go down. In self-defense, he returned fire. The deputy grabbed his shoulder and fell to his knees.

Luna shouted, *"RUPEE, WAIT …!"* But it was too late.

The cricketer tried to climb into the flatbed but was met by a karate kick from the Asian woman. Rupee fell backwards. He got to his feet, but not for long. A full round of law enforcement fire sent Rupee finally tumbling to the road. Luna and Lono ran over.

Luna kneeled over the squirming, blood-soaked criminal cricketer. Rupee seemed to settle down at the sight and looked up into her eyes. "L-Luna," he called. She leaned closer. "Can you believe we once… kissed?"

"The bomb: Is it set to go off?" was all Luna wanted to know.

Rupee coughed up blood. "...would have been, had the policemen not shot... I could—millions—would've been rich, if not for you, bitch! It was...so not cricket."

Luna stiffened. "Game over, Rupee. Looks like you've timed out!" she sneered back at the cricketer. The life drained from Rupee's eyes, and Luna stood. She looked down into the valley and out toward the distant ocean. "I got "the bad guys" too, not just you. Do you hear that, Nani?" Luna whispered, hoping her words would be carried by the winds to Oahu.

The sheriff calmed his injured deputy and called into his shoulder radio for ambulance response. Meanwhile, the Asian woman with the Geiger counter approached. "Ms. Nightcrow?"

"Yes?" Luna answered her.

"The bomb: It wasn't set to detonate," the woman, who it turned out was Chinese, reported.

Lono looked suspiciously at her. "Who are you?" he asked.

"Homeland Security, sir," was the only answer Lono received.

Probably a N.E.S.T. (Nuclear Emergency Search Team) agent, Luna thought. But she had a more important question. "What about leaks?" she asked.

"I read no spillage." The agent breathed a sigh of relief. "We were lucky," she said.

"It wasn't luck, but a damned good hunch!" Lono said, looking Luna's way.

She grinned and responded, "You mean intuition, a woman's intuition?"

CHAPTER 30

Prisoner in Paradise

After 10 hours of debriefing (by what seemed like every local, state, and federal law enforcement agency and those representing India) Luna and Lono were congratulated and finally released. The "nuking for diamonds" incident was declared classified by both countries, and didn't make the news. But Rupee Sabal's death (officially caused by "evading a routine attempt for information pertaining to the whereabouts of Pacific Splendor"); then, the public release of the salting scam and ICE taking the heat; and the ongoing mystery of the red diamond's current location were plenty for the mainstream and conspiracy media to gnaw on.

When Luna and Lono walked outside the Honolulu Federal Building, it was morning. "After all that, they still might need us for trial!" Luna laughed.

"Then it looks like you're a prisoner in paradise," Lono told her.

"Correction: I'm a prisoner in Honolulu," the insurance investigator snorted. "If I'm going to be "a prisoner in paradise," then I want to be *in paradise!*"

Lono smiled. "Somewhere where the coffee flows free?"

"Only if it's the Kona variety," Luna said with a wink.

CHAPTER 31

Parting Gift

Lono dropped Luna by Nani's house. She called Safe Pacific, briefed the board of directors on the outcome, and gave her recommendations. Afterward, the matter of payment came up. Luna knew that the Safe Pacific brass would be unwilling to live up to the promise to pay her 3 percent of the value of the diamond. And why should they? It was enhanced beyond its real value.

Lono estimated the diamond's worth to be $20,000. But, to keep from being paid a measly 10 or 20 percent of that, Luna boldly asked, "How about $50,000 as fair pay? It's what I'd probably make in a year, as an experienced insurance investigator, for most companies."

Considering what she'd sacrificed for them and saved them, the board collectively agreed. They even asked if she wanted to head their Special Investigations Unit. Luna politely declined, thinking about how careless Safe Pacific hiring and supervisory practices allowed the likes of Nani Nyoko and Miguel Diamante to hatch the con in the first place. Luna did promise the board of directors a full written report and hung up.

Luna thought about Nani again. She was a crook. Still, Luna felt sorry for her. She was a good woman, but one without the same means as you, Luna told herself. Without your drive, style, and smarts, wouldn't you eventually give in, too? Besides, there's that custom that says you still owe Nani something for her hospitality.

So, Luna took out her pen and checkbook. She kissed her fingertips, touched them on the check she wrote, and placed it within a small card that read, "Forgot to give you a gift upon entering your home, Nani." Luna hoped $50,000 would help pay Nani's bills, if not her bail, so that the jewelry appraiser could pay for her own defense (if she didn't plea bargain).

When Luna checked her e-mail and voice mail on the laptop, dozens of requests for interviews about the Pacific Splendor case and crop fraud case poured out. Normally, it would all bring on another headache. Instead, Luna smiled and thought of which networks or magazines to grant exclusives to. And, there were still standing offers from various Risk Management Agencies for her help with uncovering crop fraud. She had plenty of ways to recoup the donated $50,000.

So, looking out the window and seeing Lono's black as licorice SUV made Luna think, *Breathe! You're in Hawaii!* Quickly, she changed out of her white skirt suit and into shorts, flip-flops, and a T-shirt. She then crammed everything into her suitcase and rolling duffel bag, scooped up the card with the check, and left.

Lono followed Luna to the hospital. After she dropped off the check and house key for Nani, Luna drove to Hertz (where she returned her rental car). Then, she loaded her bags in the back of Lono's Lincoln Navigator and climbed in the front seat.

Lono's jaw dropped at the sight of his more casual passenger.

Luna liked his admiring look and said, "Someone told me to "breathe": We're in Hawaii."

"Not yet," Lono advised.

Luna smiled, reclined, and put her feet up, as Lono geared up. Thirty minutes later, they made the highway turn-off for Honolulu International Airport. It wouldn't be long before the weight of the world would be swept away by the whirling twin engines of a familiar Piper Mojave.

CHAPTER 32

Pacific Splendor

An hour later, Lono and Luna touched down in paradise (The Big Island). After renting a car and checking into the Hale Kona Kai Condos, they dropped by the Kailua-Kona Pier for a swim. That night, Luna was treated to her first luau. The next day, it was off to Waikoloa Beach up the coast for snorkeling and surfing lessons in the bay. Then one day, a thunderstorm soaked Kona country. Luna and Lono found themselves confined to their condo, as it rained on and off into the night.

"YAHTZEE!" Luna squealed and clapped with delight, as she beat Lono at the dice game twice.

"This's the side of you that I thought I'd never see," Lono said tenderly.

"And I thought that, in Hawaii, the only fire I'd see would be from a volcano erupting!" Luna laughed, as she watched the bare-chested Hawaiian toss another log into the fireplace. "In my business,

Lono, you can't relax like this for too long. Someone might take advantage of you."

With that, levity led to lamenting. "How do you go on like that, Luna? I mean, always suspicious, always watching your back?"

Luna shrugged. "It pays to be cautious. Sometimes, Lono, it pays *very* well."

"It's all about the dollar bills, huh?"

"And paying my bills," Luna added.

"No real love for what you do, Luna?"

"For now, Lono, I'm happy to see others happy that I kept them from being conned."

Lono returned to Luna's side. "Speaking of that," he said softly, "do you think anyone will ever find Pacific Splendor?"

After a long silence, Luna looked Lono in the eye. "I've already found it," she whispered.

"*Where?!*" Lono really wanted to know.

"Right here...with you," Luna laughed.

"*Why you...!*" Lono pelted Luna with a pillow. She fought back with her own bop. After the second whack, Luna tackled Lono. "Okay, okay! I'm licked, Luna!" Lono surrendered.

"Not yet, sport!" Luna breathed, reaching for the zipper on Lono's shorts.

"*E Hoomau Maua Kealoha,*" Lono said.

Luna stopped at the sound of Hawaiian being spoken. "Please tell me what it means, Lono!" she begged.

Lono reached up and caressed Luna's lips. "May our love last forever," he said softly.

Luna smiled. "Right now, I'll settle for *love-making* instead," she said.

Luna straddled Lono's smooth barrel chest; wet her lips; and, at last, locked her captive in a hungering stare. Lono grinned, as his shorts and Luna's top came off, because soon the love-making would be on.